BEST FR

Kathryn Cave is the au... books for children of a... Oxford and then Massachusetts Institute of Technology. Both as a girl and as an adult she spent long periods in America and has also lived in Australia. She was a freelance editor before she turned to writing. Kathryn Cave lives in West London and is married with three children.

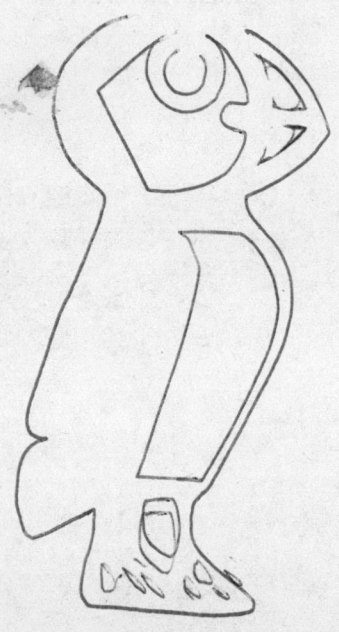

By the same author

DRAGONRISE

HENRY HOBBS, ALIEN

RUNNING BATTLES

WILLIAM AND THE WOLVES

For younger readers

JUMBLE

POOR LITTLE MARY

Best Friends For Ever

Kathryn Cave

Illustrated by
Derek Brazell

PUFFIN BOOKS

PUFFIN BOOKS

Published by the Penguin Group
Penguin Books Ltd, 27 Wrights Lane, London W8 5TZ, England
Penguin Books USA Inc., 375 Hudson Street, New York, New York 10014, USA
Penguin Books Australia Ltd, Ringwood, Victoria, Australia
Penguin Books (NZ) Ltd, 182–190 Wairau Road, Auckland 10, New Zealand

Penguin Books Ltd, Registered Offices: Harmondsworth, Middlesex, England

First published by Viking 1994
Published in Puffin Books 1995
1 3 5 7 9 10 8 6 4 2

Text copyright © Kathryn Cave, 1994
Illustrations copyright © Derek Brazell, 1994
All rights reserved

The moral right of the author has been asserted

Printed in England by Clays Ltd, St Ives plc

Except in the United States of America, this book is sold subject
to the condition that it shall not, by way of trade or otherwise, be lent,
re-sold, hired out, or otherwise circulated without the publisher's
prior consent in any form of binding or cover other than that in
which it is published and without a similar condition including this
condition being imposed on the subsequent purchaser

For Alice, Katy and Vikki

One

Sam and Alex had been friends since their first day in Mrs Parker's class.

First they were friends by accident.

Sam sat down next to Alex on the carpet that first morning, and they turned out to be wearing the same socks. Alex noticed before Sam did. He gave Sam a nudge, waved his feet about and grinned.

Sam thought a bit, and then he grinned back.

Next they were friends because they had something in common: they were the only ones in Mrs Parker's class who couldn't skip.

'The only ones in the class?' Alex grumbled after one disastrous PE lesson. 'We're the only ones on the planet, that's what. We're the only people in the whole solar system who can't skip.'

'What about martians?' asked Sam, frowning.

'Of course martians can skip. They're martians! It stands to reason.'

'You're right, then,' Sam said, depressed. 'It's only us.'

He and Alex spent hours practising together with Sam's sister Diane's skipping-rope. The practice was meant to be a deadly secret but somehow people found out. They started turning up to watch, first in ones and twos, then in large groups.

'You're supposed to *jump* the rope, not tread on it,' Mary pointed out, watching critically from the sidelines.

Amanda nodded. She was the tiniest person in the whole school, but she could skip backwards and forwards, and do all sorts of fancy things involving crossed arms and hopping.

'I'll show you, shall I?' Amanda reached out for the skipping-rope.

Alex held on to it like a limpet. 'No! Go away!'

Eventually Amanda and Mary went off to play with Kate. That just left Albert, and Sasha, and Pete and Michael, and half a dozen others.

'You jump too late,' Pete said after Sam's turn at skipping. 'Try jumping sooner.'

So Sam tried.

'Oh dear, oh dear.' Pete shook his head. 'That was *too* soon.'

Sam gave him a bitter look, untangled himself, and handed the rope to Alex.

When Alex tried to skip, the rope kept hitting the ground.

'You should hold your hands higher,' Michael said.

'How high? Like this?' Alex asked eagerly. 'Is this high enough? Oh!'

They peered up at the rope, dangling from the branches of the cherry tree.

'That was too high, really,' said Michael, as Albert went to borrow a chair from Mrs Parker.

Sam and Alex learned to skip quite suddenly a week later, when no one was watching, but they went on being friends anyway, because by then they really liked each other.

Two years on, they were still friends. Every morning Sam sat next to Alex while their teacher, Mr Dixon, read out names from the register.

Every lunch-time, Alex sat next to Sam in the dining-hall.

Every playtime (just about) they played space monsters with each other in the playground. It was their best game and they always played it together.

'Who did you play with today?' Sam's mother used to ask at first, before she knew the answer. 'Pete? Albert? Sasha?'

'Alex,' Sam answered day after day, week after week, month after month. 'I played with Alex.'

'I don't believe this,' said Sam's sister as they walked home one afternoon in March. She was ten by then, and Sam was eight. 'Don't you and Alex ever get fed up with each other? Don't you ever quarrel?'

'Why should we?' asked Sam. 'We've got nothing to quarrel about.'

Diane clicked her tongue impatiently. '*That* doesn't matter.' She was always quarrelling with her best friend Ruth, and making up, and quarrelling again. Where quarrels were concerned, she was a real expert. 'People don't quarrel *about* things. They just quarrel. It'll happen to you and Alex one day. I mean, I expect even Sarah and I will quarrel some time.'

Sam's mother had been walking in front with his little sister Laura, who was telling a complicated story about a hippopotamus. The story had been going on for longer than Sam could remember. Months? *Years?* Every now and then his mother's voice floated back to him, saying things like 'Really?' and 'That's nice.'

Suddenly she stopped right in the middle of the pavement (so suddenly that Sam walked straight into her).

'Sarah?' said his mother. '*Sarah?*' She stared at Diane. 'Who's this Sarah? I thought you were best friends with Ruth?'

Diane rolled her eyes. 'That was ages ago, Mum. We quarrelled. Sarah's new. I've been best friends with her for two weeks now. Well, a week anyway.'

Laura pulled the sleeve of Sam's red anorak. 'Do you know what the hippomapotamus did next?'

'No. What did you quarrel with Ruth about?'

11

Sam asked Diane.

'Do you *want* to know what the hippomapotamus did next?' Laura asked.

Diane answered Sam sharply over Laura's head: 'I didn't quarrel with Ruth. She quarrelled with me.'

'How?' Sam and his mother asked simultaneously.

'Well,' said Diane. 'It's a bit complicated, actually. *She* said — No, that wasn't it. It was something she *did*. No, I remember, it was something she *tried* to do.' Diane frowned and broke off. 'Oh, what does it matter what it was? It's not important. We quarrelled. Best friends don't last for ever. And I like Sarah better anyway.'

Her mother looked at her. Then she said 'I see,' in a careful voice, which meant that she didn't.

'Guess what the hippomapotamus did next!' Laura shouted, tugging the sleeve of Diane's coat this time.

'It fell under a bus,' said Diane impatiently. 'No, it didn't. It was so bored by being in your boring story that it threw itself under the bus rather than go on living a moment longer. Then they scraped it off the road and fed it to the lions. All right?'

'Diane!' said her mother. 'I want a word with you when we get home.' She seized Laura's hand and marched off.

Laura lagged behind, gazing wistfully back at

Diane and Sam. 'Did the lions like it?' she asked. 'What were the lions called?' Next moment she started on a new story about a lion called Philip.

Sam groaned. 'You've done it now,' he told Diane. 'Philip! We'll never hear the last of it. And I don't believe what you said about quarrelling. I like Alex better than anyone in the world. We'll never quarrel.'

Diane shook her head and looked down her nose at Sam. She had a good nose for looking down. 'You just wait. You'll quarrel with Alex or he'll quarrel with you. It'll happen before the end of term, bet you anything.'

'Done!' cried Sam. '10p?'

'Make it 50p,' Diane said, a far-away gleam in her eye. 'I need 50p to get a new pair of sunglasses for Easter.'

'And I need 50p more to buy that model aeroplane,' Sam said happily.

They shook hands on the deal.

'Come on, you two,' their mother called. 'Laura wants to tell you all about Philip. Hurry up!'

'Maybe I won't buy an aeroplane after all,' Sam thought dreamily. 'Maybe I'll just carry the 50p around in my pocket for a week or two and enjoy being wealthy.'

'Maybe I'll put it in the Post Office?' Diane thought. 'Or my savings box? Or my running-

away-from-home fund?' It was a difficult decision, and there was no hurry.

First came the little matter of encouraging a quarrel between Sam and Alex. How did quarrels *happen*?

'Why are you frowning like that?' Diane's mother asked as she opened the front gate. 'Is something the matter?'

'Oh, nothing,' Diane said vaguely. 'Just thinking.'

Two

Over the next week, Diane bided her time, waiting for the chance to nudge Sam into quarrelling with Alex. It wasn't as easy as it ought to have been.

Sometimes she found herself wondering if Sam was quite — well — normal.

For example, when she pointed out that Alex was taller than Sam, even though he was three weeks younger, Sam just said 'I know.'

'Don't you *mind*?' Diane asked, flabbergasted.

'Not really.' He didn't even glance up from his comic.

Five minutes later, Diane tried again. This time she said Alex was cleverer than Sam was.

'Yes, but I'm better at spelling,' Sam said cheerfully.

There was no point asking if he minded Alex being cleverer, because it was so obvious that he didn't.

What was wrong with the boy?

'And Alex is braver than you,' Diane said in desperation. 'And nicer-looking.'

At last Sam looked up from his comic. 'Do you think so?' he said slowly.

'Everybody thinks so,' Diane replied.

Sam cleared his throat. 'Do you fancy Alex or

something?' he asked delicately. 'I always thought –'

'For heaven's sake!' Diane said. 'Me – fancy Alex? You're joking!'

'– you fancied William Bennet.'

'I do not!' Diane shouted. She stamped out of the room in a very bad temper. But she didn't give up.

On the second-to-last day of term, Sam came out into the playground after lunch to play space monsters with Alex. The current version of the game involved a fair bit of swooping round the playground shouting 'nyugga nyugga' or 'gloop gloop'. (There was a lot more to space monsters than that, of course, but only Sam or Alex could tell you what.)

Sam was carrying out a routine probe of deepest space when he encountered a large field of meteorites beneath Mrs Parker's window. Dodging them at high speed, he ran smack into Diane as she came down the steps from the dining-hall.

'Look where you're going, twit,' Diane said, rubbing her elbow. 'That hurt! You almost knocked me and Sarah over!'

It's a handicap for a space monster, having a sister. Still, Sam said 'Nyugga nyugga,' by way of apology, before turning around to swoop off again.

'Wait!' Diane grabbed hold of his jumper. It had suddenly come to her that if she couldn't persuade Sam to quarrel with Alex, she'd have to work on Alex instead. Which meant tracking him down — no easy task in a playground thronged with approximately 150 children. 'Where's Alex?'

Sam strained forward but he couldn't escape. He twisted round to glare at Diane over his shoulder. 'Nyugga! Nyugga!'

Sarah edged away. 'Is that your brother, Diane? Why does he keep saying that?'

'Talk English,' Diane growled, trying unsuccessfully to tug Sam out of earshot. He was small but solid. 'People will think you're batty. I don't want them thinking I've got a batty brother.'

'Nyugga!' the space monster said with cold defiance, and freed himself with a sudden desperate wriggle. As he raced off in triumph, a mousy girl with plaits came out of the dining-hall and drifted towards Diane.

'Ruth!' said Diane, very much surprised.

'What do *you* want?' Sarah demanded.

Ruth looked at Diane. 'Thought you might want to play.'

'Well . . .' Diane began.

'You can't play with us,' Sarah told Ruth firmly. 'The game we're playing is just for two.' She looked at Diane. 'That's right, isn't it?'

'Well . . .' Diane said again.

'There you are!' said Sarah. 'Sorry, Ruth.'

She didn't sound sorry.

'Sorry, Ruth,' Diane said.

As a matter of fact, she *was* sorry. Before she and Ruth had quarrelled, she'd really liked her. Even now, she didn't *not* like her.

Ruth drifted away towards the football field. 'Tell you what,' Sarah called after her. 'We might play a game for three tomorrow. Maybe. Come and ask, all right?'

Ruth went on walking.

'Don't suppose we *will* want to play a game for three tomorrow,' Sarah told Diane cosily. 'I was only being polite. Come on, I want to play hopscotch.'

'All right – oh!' At just that moment Diane caught sight of Alex orbiting the netball post at the other end of the playground. 'Wait a minute. I've got to give someone a message.'

Sarah frowned. 'But I want to play hopscotch.'

'It won't take a minute. We'll still have time.'

'But I want to play hopscotch *now*.'

'I'll be as quick as I can,' Diane called as she set off.

'You'd better be!' Sarah called back.

*

'Alex,' said Diane in her friendliest voice, 'can I speak to you for a moment?'

'Gloop gloop?' Alex said before hurtling on.

Next time he came round, Diane said: 'I want to talk to you about Sam –'

'Gloooop!' said Alex. 'Gloo-oo-oop!' Then he was off again, faster than ever.

Diane's head was beginning to spin. 'Can't you stand still for a minute?'

'Gloop.'

That seemed to mean no.

Diane sighed and soldiered on. 'Sam thinks you ought –'

'Gloop!'

'To play with other people sometimes –'

'Gloopoopooop!'

'– so why don't you ask Pete to play space monsters with you instead?' said Diane very quickly.

Alex stopped and looked at her with a puzzled expression. 'Gloop?' he said in a doubtful voice.

'Pete's just over there with Michael. Look –'

'Nyugga nyugga!' a familiar voice cried in Diane's ear. She looked round and there was Sam, safe back from his battle with meteorites, beaming from ear to ear.

'Gloop!' cried Alex.

The two space monsters raced away in search of new planets.

Diane watched sourly. Some people, she couldn't help thinking, were just too stupid to quarrel. She made her way back to the dining-hall doorway.

Amy and Natasha were sitting on the steps, talking. 'Have you seen Sarah anywhere?' asked Diane.

Amy nodded. 'She went off to play hopscotch.'

'With Ruth,' added Natasha.

'She can't have done!' Diane cried. 'She was going to play with me. She doesn't even like Ruth! You must be wrong!'

'Go and see, then,' Amy said reasonably.

The hopscotch game was painted in one corner of the playground. Diane ran all the way there. And there, sure enough, was Sarah, with Ruth, playing a game of hopscotch.

Diane waited until it was Ruth's turn, and then she went over to Sarah. 'Can I play too?' she asked.

Sarah shook her head. 'Hopscotch is no good with three.'

'You could play with me instead of Ruth,' said Diane. 'You were going to play with me. You said you would.' She tried hard not to sound upset.

'Maybe I'll play with you tomorrow,' Sarah said in a kindly voice. 'If Ruth and I aren't playing something different. I've had enough hopscotch

now. Do you want to share my crisps, Ruth?'

Sarah and Ruth walked off arm-in-arm.

'Come and ask if you can play with us tomorrow,' Sarah called over her shoulder. 'OK?'

Diane was too upset to answer.

Three

Term ended the next day.

After school finished, Sam went to wait for Diane outside her classroom. She came out last, blowing her nose.

'Can I have the 50p now?' he asked the moment she was out of the door. 'Alex and I haven't quarrelled. I knew we wouldn't. Can I have the money now, so I can spend it?' There was a model shop on the way home. He could drop in and buy the aeroplane.

Diane didn't say anything. When he looked at her again, Sam saw that her cheeks were shiny and she had red eyelids.

'What's the matter?' he asked. 'Is something wrong?'

'What do *you* think?' she said, and headed for the school gate without waiting for an answer.

Her mother was at the gate with Laura. 'Where's Sarah?' she asked Diane. 'I thought she was coming home with you today.'

'Well, she isn't.'

Her mother looked puzzled. 'But you told me –'

'I'm not speaking to Sarah!' said Diane in a fierce voice.

On the way home, it turned out that she wasn't

speaking to Amy either. Or Natasha, or Katherine, or Suzanne.

'Or Ruth?' Sam asked, just checking.

'Of course I'm not speaking to Ruth!' Diane shouted. 'I haven't been speaking to her all term. Why doesn't anyone listen to me!' She burst into tears.

'Diane's crying,' Laura said with surprise. Her chin began to wobble.

'I'm not crying!' sobbed Diane.

'Oh, Diane,' her mother said in a funny voice. 'Goodness me, Laura! There's no need for you to start crying too. You're sad about *which* hippopotamus? Oh, for heaven's sake!'

It wasn't the moment to mention the model aeroplane.

By the time they got home, even Sam felt gloomy. Diane pounded up the stairs to her bedroom, and slammed her door. When Sam went to ask very politely for the 50p, she told him to go away.

'I haven't got it anyway!' she said. 'I bought a big bag of sweets to share with Sarah, and she took *twelve* and she *still* said I couldn't play with her.'

'She's horrible then,' Sam said.

Diane flung herself down with her face in the pillow. If she'd been Laura, Sam would have known what to say, but Diane was more difficult.

'Forget the 50p,' he said eventually. 'I'm sorry about Sarah.'

Diane curled up into a ball with her back to him. '*I'm* not sorry. I hate Sarah. I'm glad I'm not friends with her any more.'

'Oh!'

Sam went away, shutting the door softly behind him.

Over dinner, Diane hardly said a word. What with her, and Laura mourning her squashed hippopotamus, it was a sombre evening.

Next morning they were off to spend a week by the sea. The flat they were renting had only three bedrooms, and Sam ended up sharing with Laura. She told a grim story about Philip and a lost rabbit for half the night, and snored the other half. Sam's mother said it was because Laura was worried about starting school after the holiday, and that everyone had to be very patient.

'She hasn't even *got* a rabbit,' complained Sam, hollow-eyed from lack of sleep. 'And if she did have a rabbit, chances are Mrs Parker would let her bring it to school with her. They let you bring anything to school in the infants. What's she worrying about lost rabbits for?'

'Yes,' agreed Diane. 'She should be telling stories

about Philip not having anyone to play with and horrible lunches and falling over in the playground and being told off by Mr Elliot for forgetting your PE bag and being shouted at by Mrs Hotchkiss. That's the sort of thing she needs to worry about. Not rabbits!'

Sam's mother said it was a bit hard to explain, but it was definitely all to do with starting school, and they had to be very understanding.

'And anyone who so much as mentions falling over or being told off by whoever-it-was loses a week's pocket money,' added Sam's father. 'Understand that, Diane? You too, Sam? And don't mention that wretched lion, either. She might forget him in a few days if we all keep quiet.'

Sam and Diane exchanged looks. Some hope.

'Why does it have to be me who shares with her, then?' asked Sam, polishing off his cornflakes. 'Why can't Diane have a turn?'

'Because I'm oldest,' Diane said smugly.

It was no use trying to argue that one.

After breakfast, Diane went out with her father to buy postcards to send Amy and Katherine and Natasha (but not Sarah, who she wasn't going to speak to ever again). Sam went too, to buy just one card, to send Alex.

When they arrived back, Laura was sitting on the sofa with a far-away expression on her face, eating a slice of bread and Marmite. 'Do you know what Philip eats for breakfast?' she asked Sam.

'Hippopotamuses?' Sam suggested before he could stop himself. 'Oh, sorry!'

'Would you like some more bread and Marmite, Laura?' his mother said loudly. The look she sent Sam had 'no pocket money' written all over it.

'Why on earth should Philip eat hippopotamuses?' Sam's father asked, baffled.

'He doesn't!' Sam's mother said, exasperated.

Laura burst into tears. 'He does! He eats three of them every day for breakfast. Squashed hippomapotamus is his favourite food.'

'I give up,' Sam's father reached for the paper. Diane sat down beside him and spread out her cards on the table.

Her mother looked up from comforting Laura. 'What about writing to Ruth?' she asked.

Diane shook her head and looked stubborn. 'She's best friends with Sarah now. Sarah said so.'

'That doesn't mean it's true, does it?' her mother asked.

She got a withering look in reply.

'Was that why you quarrelled with Sarah?' asked Sam. 'Because she wanted to be best friends with Ruth?'

He got a withering look too.

'I was only asking.'

Sam took his card from his pocket. 'Dear Alex,' he wrote at the top, 'This is where I am.' He was just adding, 'Your friend Sam,' at the bottom, when Diane gave a cry.

'Bother!'

'Bother!' said Laura.

Sam's mother sighed. 'What's the matter, Diane?'

'I've written "Ruth" on this card instead of "Amy".' Diane glared at her mother and Sam. 'It's your fault. I wouldn't have done it if everyone hadn't been going on about her. Now I'll have to throw it away!'

She tore up the card and stalked out to the kitchen. Sam heard the bin-flap open and shut.

'You could still have sent it,' her mother said when Diane returned. 'You always used to send Ruth a card.'

'I don't *want* to, all right?' Diane shouted, picking up her second card.

Sam turned his attention to Alex's address. He was just trying to squeeze in 'The Universe' beneath 'England, Europe, The World' when Laura appeared at his elbow.

'Who can I send my card to?' she asked anxiously.

'Dunno,' Sam said. 'What about what's-his-name, the one with the ears? Malcolm?'

Laura looked thoughtful.

'Everyone's got ears, Sam,' his mother said with disapproval.

'Not like Malcolm's,' Sam argued. 'Malcolm's ears aren't just ears. They're *ears*. What? Oh, sorry!'

'I don't like Malcolm,' Laura stated.

'You do!' Sam's mother protested. 'He's your best friend.'

'I hate Malcolm!' Laura said passionately. 'We had a terrible, terrible quarrel —'

'What about?' asked Sam, trying to retrieve the situation.

'A rabbit.' Laura's chin wobbled. 'I'm never going to speak to him again. I'm never going to speak to *anyone*.'

'Good!' said Diane crossly, throwing her pen down on the table. 'I was just telling Natasha that we saw a seal yesterday, and because of you I put rabbit. Now I might as well tear this up too. These cards cost 40p, you know.'

'We *could* have seen a rabbit,' Sam pointed out, trying to make the best of things.

'Not one as big as a dog, swimming in the harbour!' Diane wailed.

Sam's father started laughing, and so did Laura. Even Diane joined in eventually.

They put away the postcards and went for a walk on the beach.

*

On their last night away, Sam's mother gave him and Diane a long talk in the kitchen after Laura was in bed. What it boiled down to was that Laura was their sister and they had to look after her.

'I know she's my sister,' Sam said, aggrieved. 'You don't have to tell me. I'm sharing a room with her, remember?'

Diane sniffed, and said that no one had looked after *her* at school, which naturally led Sam to say that no one had looked after him either.

'What?' said Diane. '*What?*'

'About Laura...' Sam's mother said patiently. 'All I mean is —'

'Who exactly are you claiming didn't look after you at school?' Diane went on, looking at Sam.

'No one — no, I mean everyone,' Sam was getting confused. 'You know what I mean.'

'Well!' said Diane. '*Really!*' At this point Sam's mother gave up and went to watch television. Sam stayed behind to discover that somebody *had* looked after him at school after all, and that person was Diane!

'You?' Sam was astonished. He might even have been flabbergasted. 'Are you sure?'

That led to a long catalogue of all the things Diane had done for her brother.

She'd gone to help him up when he'd been knocked down in the playground. (Sam didn't

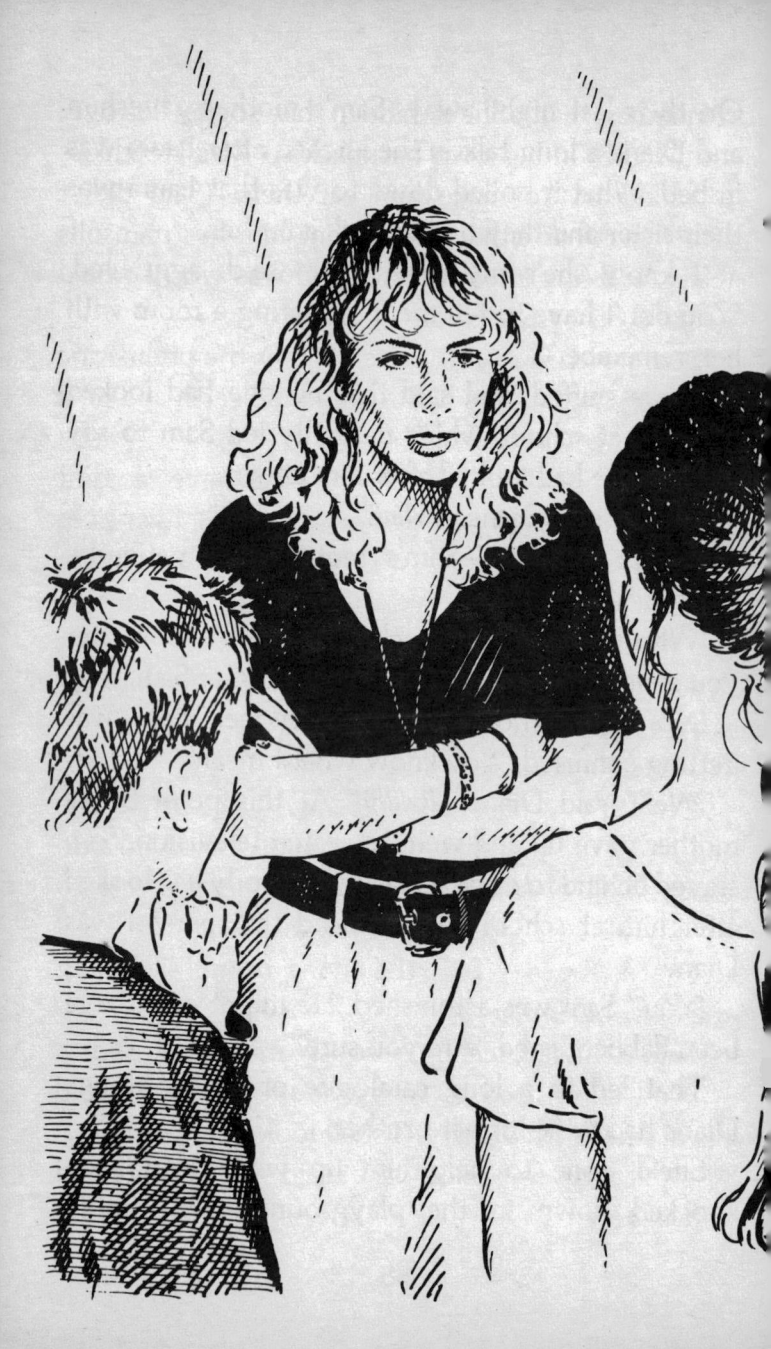

remember that.) She'd hidden his soggy leftover sandwiches in her own backpack so Mrs Hotchkiss wouldn't try to make him eat them. (Sam didn't remember that either.) She'd lent him her plimsolls when he'd forgotten his own and was worried he'd get told off by Mr Elliot.

Sam frowned, trying to remember the prehistoric days when dinosaurs had roamed the earth and he'd been in the infant school.

Now she mentioned it, he did have a faint memory of wearing a pair of plimsolls two sizes too big during a PE lesson in Mrs Parker's class. He'd tried to hop as fast as Alex, lost a plimsoll, and practically broken his neck.

He shared the memory with Diane, thinking she'd be glad he'd remembered.

Wrong again.

'Not my fault you were born clumsy,' she snarled. 'I did my best for you, and what thanks do I get? Talk about ungrateful. Don't expect me to do anything for you ever again, that's all!'

She stomped off to the living-room, slamming the door behind her.

Sam followed, feeling seriously misunderstood.

'You don't need to worry about Laura,' he told his mother with dignity. 'I shall look after her.'

'Well, try for once,' she said in a depressed sort of way.

'Him – look after Laura?' Diane scoffed. 'That'll be the day. I'll look after her, Mum. At least I know what I'm doing.'

'So do I!' Sam shouted.

'You?' Diane looked at him with scorn. 'You couldn't look after anyone. You couldn't look after a brussels sprout.'

Sam went to bed extremely cross.

Four

The first day of the summer term arrived. On the way to school, Sam's mother held one of Laura's hands and Diane held the other. Sam mooched along behind, listening to Diane tell Laura that at school she would meet kind teachers, have endless games, and eat delicious lunches.

Sam blinked. 'This is our school you're talking about?' he enquired. 'St George's?'

'Ssh!' his mother said. 'Go on, Diane.'

'What if I lose my PE bag?' Laura interrupted. She was clutching the bag to her anorak as if it had the Crown Jewels inside, rather than Sam's old painting overall and a pair of plimsolls.

'Just *don't*, that's all,' Sam said.

'Sam!' said his mother.

'It doesn't matter if you lose your bag, Laura,' Diane said without turning a hair. 'No one will mind.'

'Mr Elliot will,' said Sam. 'He'll mind all right.'

'Be quiet, Sam,' said his mother, glaring.

'None of the teachers will mind about you losing anything, Laura.' As Diane spoke, she trod heavily on Sam's right foot. 'Not even Mr Elliot.'

'That hurt!' said Sam. No one paid any attention.

Later, when Sam tried to do his bit to cheer

Laura up by asking in a brotherly way if Philip had eaten any more squashed hippopotamuses lately, Laura's chin started to wobble.

'If that's your idea of helping,' his mother said crossly, 'it's just as well Diane's going to be looking after Laura, not you.'

'He couldn't look after a brussels sprout,' said Laura through her sobs.

While Sam was still speechless, Diane wiped Laura's nose on the PE bag. 'Shall I tell you about dinner ladies, Laura?' she said cosily. 'Dinner ladies are *nice*. They're there to help us at lunch-time.'

Sam couldn't believe his ears. 'What?!'

'Not another word, Sam,' his mother said.

He reeled into school in a state of shock.

After the bell had rung, Sam was telling Alex what had happened, when Mr Dixon walked into class with someone new.

'Welcome back, everybody,' he said. 'This is Emma.' He gave Emma a friendly pat on the head. 'She's new here, and I know you're all going to be very nice to her and make her feel at home. Sam, if you're not too busy chatting to Alex, would you look after Emma until she settles in, please?'

'Me?' Sam asked. Mr Dixon had never asked him to look after anyone before. It was usually Pete or

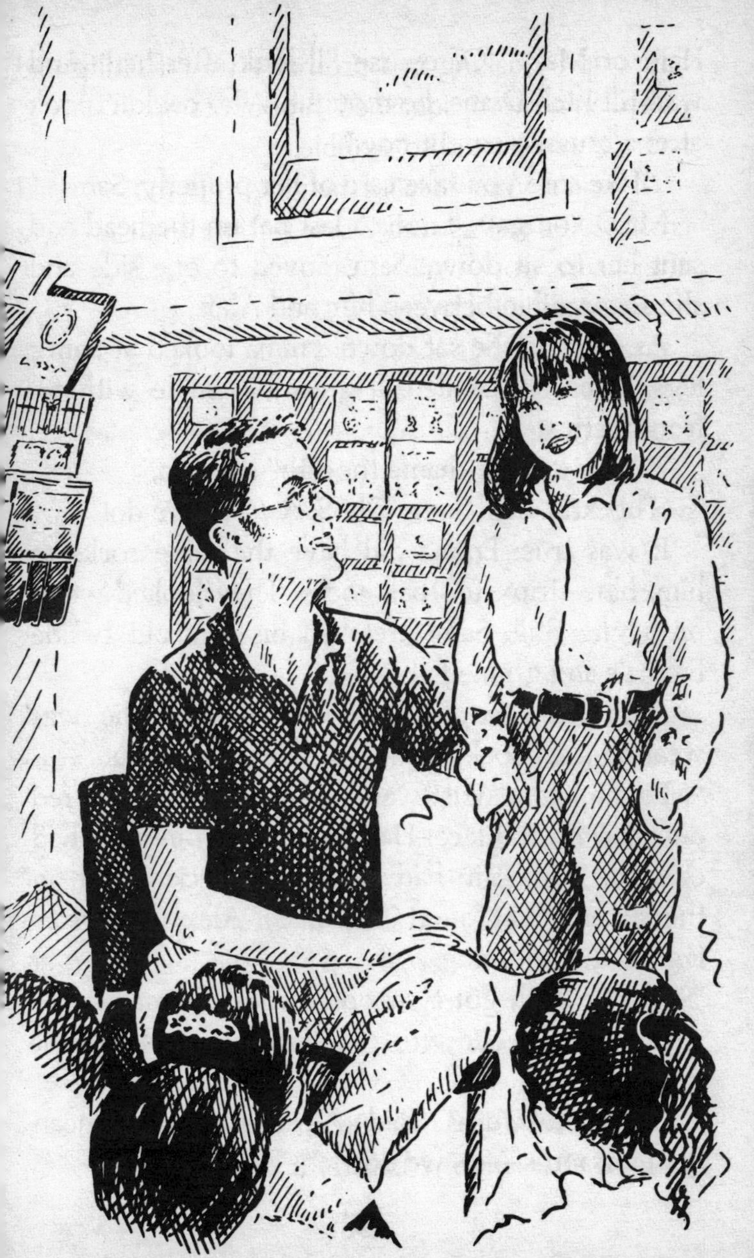

Kate or Mary. 'Of course I'll look after her!' And wait till I tell Diane, he thought. Who couldn't look after a brussels sprout now?

'Make sure you take care of her properly, Sam.'

Mr Dixon gave Emma a last pat on the head and sent her to sit down. Sam moved to one side and she squeezed in between him and Alex.

As soon as she sat down, Emma looked at Sam's legs. Then she smiled, a great big smile with no front teeth.

'We've got the thame thockth!' she said.

'Thockth?' said Sam. 'Oh! *Socks!* Yes, we do!'

It was true: Emma did have the same socks as him, blue stripy football socks. They looked weird on a girl. Still, Sam stretched his legs out beside Emma's and grinned at her.

Alex stretched his legs out too, but he was wearing grey socks so he was the odd one out.

Emma had a wrist-watch with a picture of a red dinosaur on the face. Half the children in class had one the same (it had been on special offer in the supermarket over Christmas). Alex was wearing his that morning.

'We've both got tyrannothawuth!' Emma said to Alex, waving her wrist at him. She smiled that smile again.

'Tiranno*what*uth?' said Alex. 'Oh, you mean tyrannosaurus! Yes, we do!'

Emma and Alex put their watches side by side and chuckled.

Sam wasn't wearing his watch that day. (It wasn't lost or anything. He just didn't know where it was.) Still, he cheered up when he remembered that he was the one Mr Dixon had asked to look after Emma.

At break, Sam made the supreme sacrifice. Instead of playing space monsters, he took Emma on a tour of the school.

Alex came too, grumbling.

The tour began right outside the classroom, in the children's cloakroom.

'This is the cloakroom, Emma,' Sam said.

'Yeth?' Emma looked around politely. It was a pretty ordinary cloakroom.

She looked at Sam again. 'Yeth?'

'This is where we put our coats . . .'

Sam opened his locker and pointed out his red anorak hanging inside. On the floor of the locker was a gym shoe minus its laces, and an ancient apple core which was part of an experiment Sam and Alex were doing, to see what happens to apple cores if they're left a very long time in a locker.

'Yeth,' said Emma when he had explained this carefully. 'I thee.'

Sam gave her a minute to admire the apple core and then shut the door. What else ought he to show her?

The trouble was, there wasn't much *to* show.

'That table over there is where we put our lunch-boxes. Through here ...' Sam led the way into the next room, '... are the basins where we wash our hands.'

'I thee.' Emma peered into a basin.

Alex peered too. 'Sally Platt said she found a frog in there once. Nobody else saw it, though. Mr Dixon said she imagined it. I did see a beetle once.'

There was a pause.

'Yeth?' said Emma.

'It was dead, though.'

Sam coughed. 'This is where to get a paper towel to dry your hands, Emma.'

'I think someone trod on it. Funny place to get trodden on, though. In a basin.'

'Yeth,' said Emma.

'And why was it in the basin in the first place?'

Sam was fed up with beetles, and basins. 'This is the door to the playground,' he said very loudly.

'Of course it's a door,' Alex said, sounding cross. He had just thought of how the beetle might have got into the basin, but the moment Sam interrupted, the theory vanished. 'Anyone can see a door when it's right in front of them.'

Sam felt his face go red. He led Emma out into the playground without answering and immediately tripped over a small girl with fair hair in bunches,

42

who was hopping in a circle backwards with her eyes closed.

'Ow,' said Sam crossly, picking himself up. 'Look where you're going.'

'Don't be silly,' the girl said calmly from the ground. 'How can I look where I'm going with my eyes shut? Would you like to play horrible hedgehog?'

'No!' said Sam.

'Of course not. We're not allowed to. You know that!' said Alex.

The girl looked up at Emma. 'Would *you* like to play horrible hedgehog?'

'She certainly would not,' Sam said. 'Come along, Emma.'

He marched her off towards the infant school.

'Who'th that?' Emma asked, lagging behind. 'How do you play horrible hedgehog?'

'It's Sally Platt. She's trouble,' said Sam. 'You don't want to have anything to do with her.'

Alex nodded. 'Or horrible hedgehog. It's against the rules.'

'Which ruleth?' asked Emma.

'*The* rules,' said Sam. 'Look, Emma, this is Mrs Parker's room. She takes the first infants. That's them in there now.'

Sam peered in through the classroom window. So did Alex and Emma.

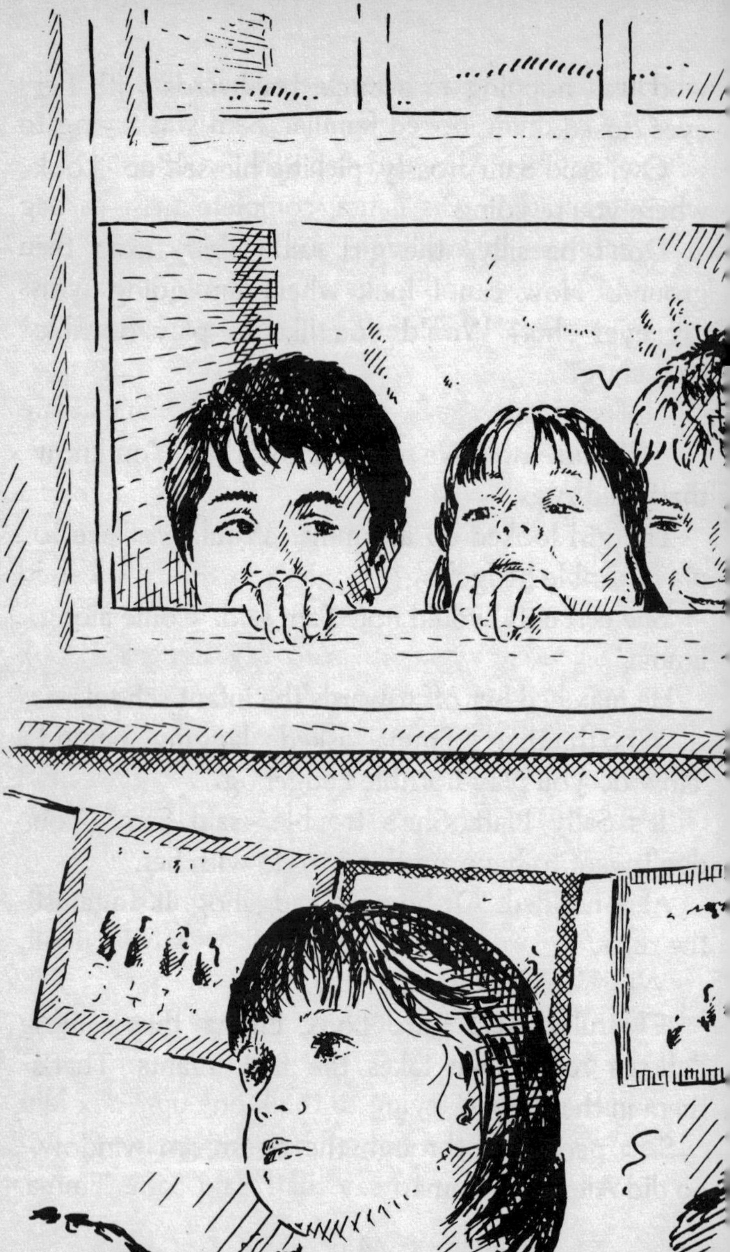

Hundreds of small faces peered back.

One of them looked familiar. Sam was trying to place her when Alex said: 'Isn't that your sister?'

Of course! It was Laura, complete with PE bag clutched to her cardigan, and wobbly chin. Sam crossed his eyes and made a face through the glass at her to show that he loved her, and Laura burst into tears.

At exactly the same moment, Sam became aware of the face of Miss Holt, the nursery helper, centimetres away on the other side of the glass.

'GO AWAY!' Miss Holt mouthed at him.

'I'll show you something else now, shall I?' said Sam quickly.

As he led the retreat, he tried to sneak a look past Miss Holt to see Laura. All he could see was the top of her head as she sobbed into her PE bag. Then Miss Holt rapped on the glass and mouthed several other things, none of them friendly.

'That wasn't Mrs Parker,' Sam said as they left, in order to say something. 'That was Miss Holt. She's different.'

'Yeth?' Emma looked expectantly at him, waiting for the punch line.

While Sam was trying to think one up, Alex lent a hand: 'Mrs Parker's got red hair and glasses.'

'I was just going to say that!' said Sam. 'Emma,

Mrs Parker has red hair and glasses. Now, this class here belongs to Mr Winch. He has . . .'

Alex had had enough. 'Vampire teeth and a laser gun!' he said, making a Dracula face.

Emma chuckled.

Before Sam could stop himself, he glared at Alex. 'I'm the one who's looking after Emma, not you. Don't keep interrupting and making stupid jokes. This is serious.'

Alex glared back. Until then, Sam had always been the first person to appreciate his jokes. 'If it's so serious, why have you missed out lots of things?' he demanded. 'You've missed out the football field. You haven't told her where the water fountain is. What if she gets thirsty? She won't know where to get a drink. I don't call that looking after someone.'

Alex stamped off to the far side of the playground by himself.

Sam marched Emma in the opposite direction. 'This classroom here is Miss Walker's,' he told her masterfully.

'Doth thee have vampire teeth?' asked Emma hopefully.

'Of course not! She's . . .' Sam racked his brains for something interesting to say about Miss Walker, but there wasn't anything. 'If you see someone who looks exactly like everyone else, that'll be Miss Walker. This is a classroom door. Emma?'

Emma was gazing at the far side of the playground. Sam looked and saw Alex kicking a stone against the wall of the dining-hall.

'He'th croth,' she said. 'Why don't you go and thay thorry?'

'*Thorry?* Oh, I see! Because I haven't done anything to feel sorry for, and because I'm looking after you,' Sam said with dignity. 'Now, what was I saying?'

Emma looked at him. 'You'd jutht told me that thith ith a door.'

'Ah! Right,' said Sam, regaining confidence. 'It's the door to Miss Walker's room. Emma, are you listening?'

She was looking over her shoulder again. She sighed. 'Yeth, Tham. I'm lithening.'

The bell rang and everyone went back into class. Sam and Emma took a long time getting there because Sam was trying to explain things.

There was a lot to explain, and it was hard to remember what he had explained and what he hadn't.

'Yeth, thothe are pegth,' said Emma obediently, 'Yeth, thothe are lockerth. You thaid that. Yeth, thothe thingth in the bathinth are tapth. Yeth, I thee.'

Mr Dixon stuck his head out of the classroom.
'Hurry up, you two. You're the last.'
'Hurry up, Emma,' said Sam.
'Yeth,' said Emma.

Five

When Sam and Emma reached the classroom, all the others were sitting down at tables. Mr Dixon was sitting on top of his desk, hunting through a folder.

Sam headed for his usual place, the seat next to Alex.

It was the only empty seat at that table. Sam moved it out to sit down — then he remembered Emma. How could he look after her if he wasn't beside her?

'I can thit over there.' Emma pointed to a table at the end of the row, where there was an empty seat. 'I don't mind, Tham. Honetht. You thit with Alekth.'

For a moment Sam hesitated. Then the echo of Diane's voice rang in his ear: 'You couldn't look after a brussels sprout.' The empty seat Emma was suggesting was next to none other than Sally Platt — the worst possible person for a new girl to sit beside. Sam couldn't let Emma make the sacrifice.

He shook his head. 'No, we'll sit together.'

'But I wouldn't *mind*, Tham —'

'No,' said Sam firmly. 'We can still sit here if someone moves.'

The other two at Alex's table were Pete and

Michael. Sam tried Michael first: 'Would you mind sitting with Sasha, so that Emma and I can sit here?' he asked. But Michael wouldn't move because he wanted to sit with Pete, and Pete wouldn't move because he wanted to sit with Michael.

'Well, Alex and Emma and I want to sit together too,' Sam said crossly. 'Don't we Alex?'

Alex had been tracing a pattern on the table with one finger. He looked up at Sam without smiling, and didn't answer.

Sam was trying to persuade Pete *and* Michael to move when Mr Dixon found what he was looking for in his folder.

'Sit down, Emma,' he said. 'Yes, you can sit right there beside Alex.'

Emma sat down in Sam's rightful seat.

'You sit down too, Sam,' said Mr Dixon. 'Yes, I know you usually sit beside Alex, but there's no room today. Find somewhere else.'

'But I'm looking after Emma,' Sam objected.

'Alex can look after her instead.'

And before Sam had the chance to veto this, Mr Dixon turned to Alex. 'Will you do that, Alex? Look after Emma until lunch-time? Emma, if you want to know anything, ask Alex. Understand, both of you?'

'Yeth,' said Emma.

'Yeth – I mean yes!' said Alex.

As soon as Mr Dixon was on the other side of the classroom refereeing an argument between Kate and Mary, Pete nudged Alex's elbow.

'I'll help look after her, if you like. I've looked after people before, hundreds of them. Millions, probably. I'll show you how.'

'That's all right –' Alex began.

'If Pete helps, can I help too?' asked Michael. 'I haven't actually looked after anyone before, but that's OK. I'm a quick learner.'

'I don't want any help, thank you,' said Alex. 'I know what to do.'

'Can I watch, then?' asked Michael. 'I'll have to look after someone myself one day, I expect. Can I watch how you do it?'

Pete laughed.

'Of course you can watch,' said Alex.

Mr Dixon made Kate change places with Sasha, to stop the argument with Mary. Then he handed round sheets of paper and tins of crayons. The class project that term was going to be health, he said. The first thing they were going to study was healthy eating.

'So I want you all to begin by drawing a picture of something you really like to eat,' Mr Dixon told them.

'He means draw something you really like to eat, Emma,' Alex said, quick as a flash.

Emma looked at him hard. 'I thee,' she said.

Michael coughed. 'You think she knows what drawing is?' he whispered loudly to Alex.

'Of course!' Alex whispered back. 'Everyone knows that!'

Michael looked unconvinced. 'How do you *know* she knows?'

'Because — look, I only said you could watch, not ask questions.'

'How about if I wrote the questions down?' Michael asked. 'No? What if I mimed them?'

Alex looked at him.

'I guess not,' Michael said, resigned. 'I guess I'll just watch, then.'

Alex turned back to Emma. 'What are you going to draw?' he asked encouragingly. 'A *carrot*? Do you *like* carrots? Oh!' Talk about weird. 'I'm going to draw a sausage,' he said. 'This is a sausage. You draw it like this, see. Shall I draw you a sausage? They make you *thick*? Oh, you mean *sick*!'

'That'th what I said.' Emma gave him another hard look. 'Thick!'

'Yes, she did say that,' Michael said helpfully. '*Thick!* I couldn't understand what she meant. I was listening. Were you listening too, Pete?'

Pete shrugged. 'I've better things to do with my time,' he said in a distant voice, 'than sit around listening to somebody make a mess of looking after someone just because they wouldn't take advice from somebody else on how to do it.'

'Good!' said Alex coldly when he'd worked that out. 'I'm not listening to you either.' He turned back to Emma. 'What are you drawing now? Another carrot? A *tomato*? But tomatoes are round! It's what? *Thkwauthed*? You only like thkwauthed tomatoth? Oh, I *see*!'

Alex was beginning to feel tired. He hadn't realized looking after somebody was such a strain on the brain. Still, if Sam could do it (not to mention Pete), so could he.

When he handed his sheet in at the end of the morning, Mr Dixon frowned. 'That's not much in the way of food, Alex. One sausage! And you haven't even coloured it in!'

'I was looking after Emma,' Alex told him. 'Wasn't I, Emma?'

He beamed in Emma's direction.

She didn't smile back. 'Yeth,' said Emma.

At lunch-time, Sam and Alex quarrelled.

There was no doubt about it: it was a genuine quarrel.

'I'm looking after Emma again now,' Sam said. That started it off.

'I am too,' said Alex.

'No you aren't!'

'Yes I am!'

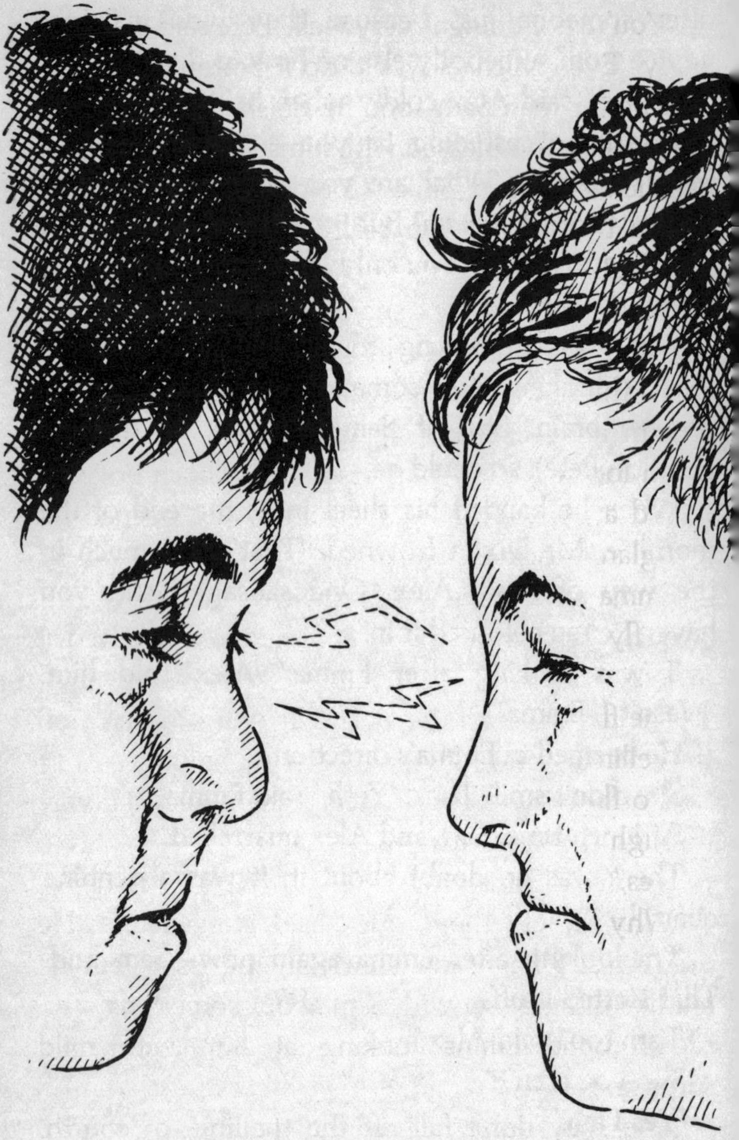

'You're not doing it very well,' Pete said disparagingly. 'Even Michael would do it better than you – and better than Sam too,' he finished, in case Sam was feeling too pleased with himself.

Michael turned pink. 'Could I really look after Emma better? Do you really think so? Can I try and see?'

'No!' Sam and Alex shouted together. 'I'm looking after Emma by myself!'

'I'll thit in the middle, thall I?' said Emma.

Sam and Alex agreed, but neither of them did much looking after. Sam opened his lunch-box and glared at Alex without speaking. Alex opened his and glared back.

Emma unwrapped her sandwich.

A fly landed on the wrapping. Alex swatted it away.

The fly rose into the air and flew up to perch on the ceiling, watched with interest by Emma.

'Do flieth have thticky feet?' she asked half-way through the sandwich.

'Yes,' said Sam.

'Why should they?' Alex said immediately. He didn't really have any views on the issue, but he felt like disagreeing with Sam about something.

He found Emma looking at him with mild surprise.

'Tho they don't fall off the theiling, of courth.

You'd fall off the theiling if you tried to walk on it.'

'Yes, I know,' said Alex, trying to retrieve his position, 'but —'

'You'd fall off the theiling and go thplat on the lino,' said Emma, very matter of fact. 'Your inthideth would come out. There'd be the motht dithguthting meth. They'd have to hothe down the wallth, probably. Don't you think tho, Tham?'

'Say that again,' said Sam, a slow translator.

Emma did.

She was the only one of the three to finish lunch.

When Emma had put her rubbish in the bin (where Sam and Alex, slightly green, had also put most of their sandwiches), she looked round the dining-hall.

On the far side of the room, Sally Platt was trying to balance her lunch-box on top of a carton of orange juice on top of an apple.

'Thall we go and talk to Thally?' said Emma wistfully.

'*Thally?* Oh, you mean Sally,' said Sam. 'No. I told you about Sally, remember? You wouldn't like her.'

Alex nodded, looking grave. 'She's always rushing up behind people in the playground and shouting.'

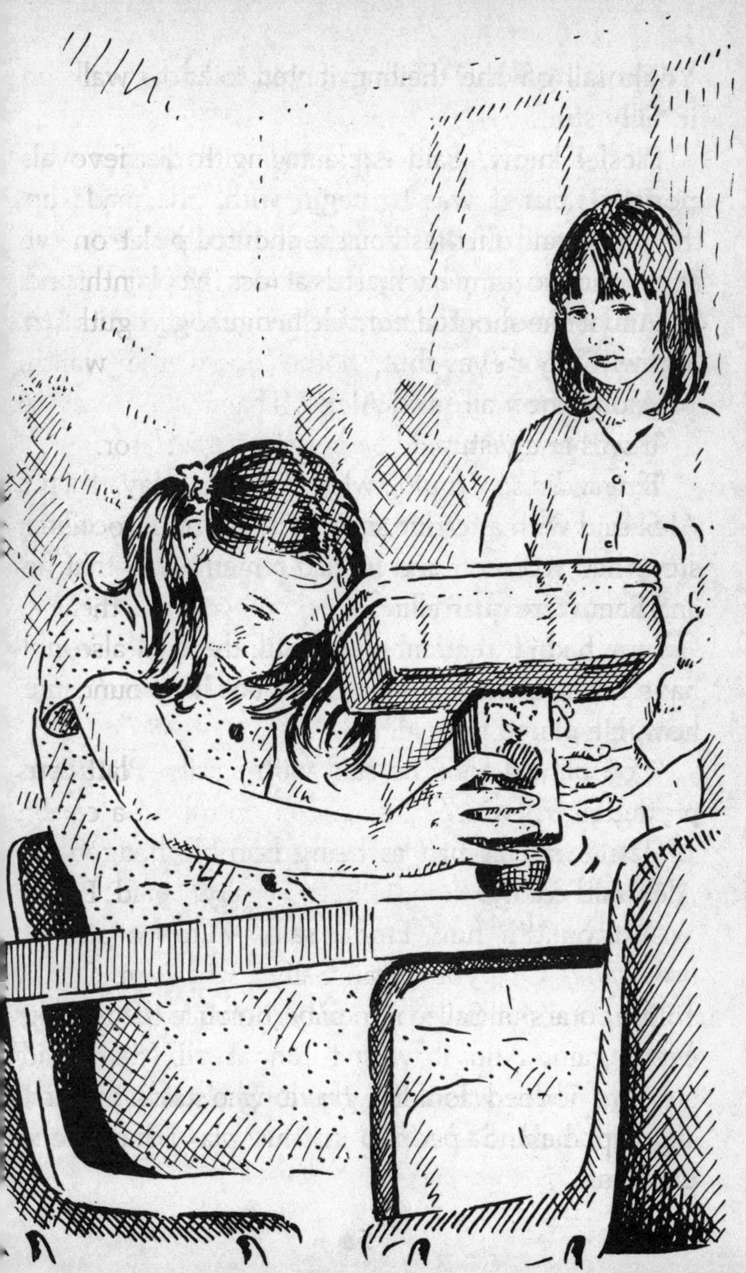

'Thouting what?' Emma wanted to know.

'Silly stuff.'

'Pickled newt,' Sam explained with disapproval. 'That's what it was to begin with. She made up this game, and if it was you she shouted pickled newt at, you had to jump backwards across the playground'

'And if she shouted horrible hedgehog you had to hop with your eyes shut.'

'Along the wall,' said Alex.

'It was really stupid.'

'If it was so stupid, why did you play, then?' Alex said with a terrific sneer. The fly-on-the-ceiling story had worn off and he had remembered that he and Sam were quarrelling.

Sam hadn't remembered until then. He would have liked to sneer back at Alex but he wasn't sure how. He glared instead.

'You played too!' he said with spirit. 'You were pickled newt twice.'

'That's not as bad as being horrible hedgehog,' Alex said coldly.

'It thoundth fun,' Emma said. 'Can we play it now?'

'No one's allowed to play horrible hedgehog ever again. And it wasn't fun at all,' Sam said sternly. 'There was a line *this* long outside the first aid cupboard. Sasha had concussion. I had three plasters.'

'*Two,*' said Alex nastily.

'All right, two. But they were big ones.'

Sam scowled at Alex and Alex scowled back.

'I thee,' said Emma vaguely. She stood up. 'Let'th go outthide anyway. I want to play thomething.'

'*Thumbthing?*' Sam scratched his ear. 'Don't think I know that game – oh, *something*! Sorry!'

Alex laughed.

Six

On the way home, Sam didn't feel like talking. This was just as well. If he'd wanted to talk, he wouldn't have been able to get a word in. His mother was trying to find out what Laura had done at school. Diane was reporting in grim detail an argument she'd had with almost everyone in her class, and Laura was explaining the various points during the day when she thought she might have lost her PE bag, but hadn't.

'Big deal,' Sam muttered, not quietly enough.

His mother gave him a pointed look. 'And what about Sam and Diane?' she asked, turning back to Laura. 'Did they look after you?'

'Nobody looked after me.' Laura looked up at her pathetically. 'Steven Maddox tried to take my PE bag in the playground after lunch and no one helped me. I *told* him to let go but he just laughed.'

'I see.' Sam's mother looked accusingly at Diane and Sam. 'And where were you two while this was happening?'

'How should I know where I was while it was happening?' Sam asked. 'I mean, I wasn't there, was I?'

'Quite,' his mother said meaningfully.

'It's hardly the crime of the century, anyway,'

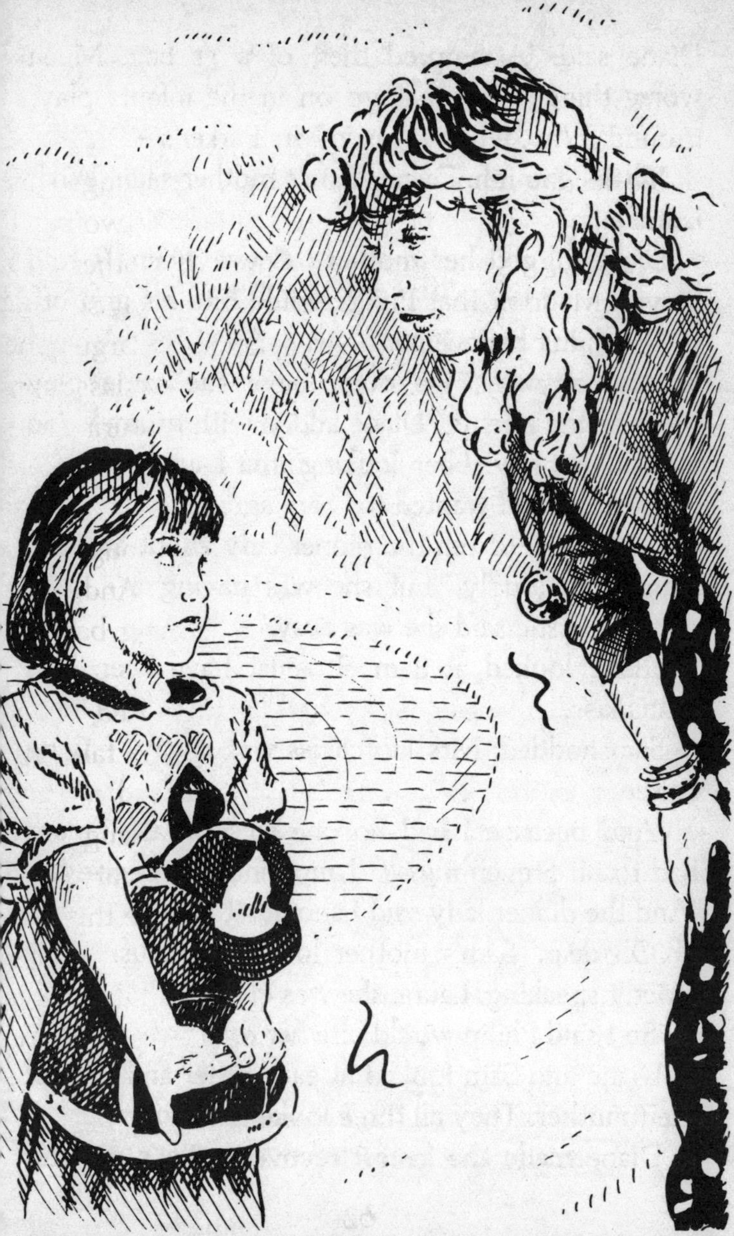

Diane said. 'Attempted theft of a PE bag. Much worse things than that go on in the infants playground. Why, when *I* was in Mrs Parker's –'

'That's enough, Diane,' Sam's mother said. 'What is it, Laura?'

Laura tugged her mother's sleeve again. 'I told Steven Maddox that Philip would bite his arm off, but he didn't believe me.'

'And anyway, we don't have the same play times as the infants,' Diane added with triumph. 'So we couldn't have been looking after Laura then.'

'Even if we'd wanted to,' Sam agreed.

'So I went to tell the dinner lady about Steven,' Laura said loudly, 'but she was having a cup of coffee and she said she was busy.'

Diane looked at Sam. 'It must have been Mrs Hotchkiss.'

Sam nodded. Mrs Hotchkiss was always having coffee.

'And because I had no one to look after me, I had to hit Steven *myself*,' Laura finished, aggrieved. 'And the dinner lady said I shouldn't have.'

'Oh dear.' Sam's mother looked anxious. 'Well, strictly speaking, Laura, she was quite ri–'

'So I said Philip would bite her too.'

Diane and Sam looked at each other and then at their mother. They all three looked at Laura.

Diane made the fastest recovery. 'Let's get this

straight,' she said. 'You told *Mrs Hotchkiss* a lion was going to bite her?'

'No!' shouted Laura. 'I said *Philip*. And she said "Who's Philip, is he your brother?"'

'That's it. I'm going to have to change schools,' Sam said in a doomed voice. 'She'll think I'm Philip and that I go round biting people. My life won't be worth living.'

'Ssh! Go on, Laura,' Diane urged.

'And I said "No, he's my pet lion who looks after me." And then I cried, and the dinner lady said I could call her Aunty Beryl and gave me a biscuit.'

'She *what*?' said Sam.

'Aunty *who*?' said Diane.

'That's enough!' said their mother, recovering her powers of speech. 'None of this would have happened if either of you had taken the least bit of trouble to look after her, the way you said you would.'

She spent the rest of the walk home telling Laura how important it was to be nice to people and *not* hit them or threaten them with being eaten by Philip. Sam spent it trying to imagine any sequence of events that might conceivably end with Mrs Hotchkiss, terror of the playground, inviting *him* to call her Aunty Beryl.

Suppose an enormous mutant octopus from outer

space crash-landed on the playing-field one lunch time, and he and Alex —

'Are you listening, Sam?' his mother demanded as they rounded the last corner. 'It's not just Laura I'm talking to.'

'You don't have to tell *me*.' Sam had remembered, rather late in the day, that he and Alex weren't even talking to each other, let alone in a position to rescue Mrs Hotchkiss from death by tentacles during the lunch-hour. '*I* don't go around beating people up. *I've* never once told someone my pet lion's going to bite their arm off. I'm normal.'

'I wouldn't say *that*,' Diane commented under her breath.

After supper, when Laura had gone to bed and Sam and Diane were helping their father clear up in the kitchen, Sam said: 'Mr Dixon asked me to look after someone new today. She's called Emma.'

'Oh?' His father peered suspiciously into a saucepan. 'Did you enjoy that?' Before Sam could answer he went on: 'What would look best in that bed at the front? Pansies or marigolds?'

Diane yawned. 'Marigolds.'

'Pansies,' said Sam. 'But then Alex said he was looking after her too.'

'Geraniums?' Then, struck by sudden inspiration, Sam's father dropped the saucepan. 'Asters!'

He picked up the saucepan and tried to put it in

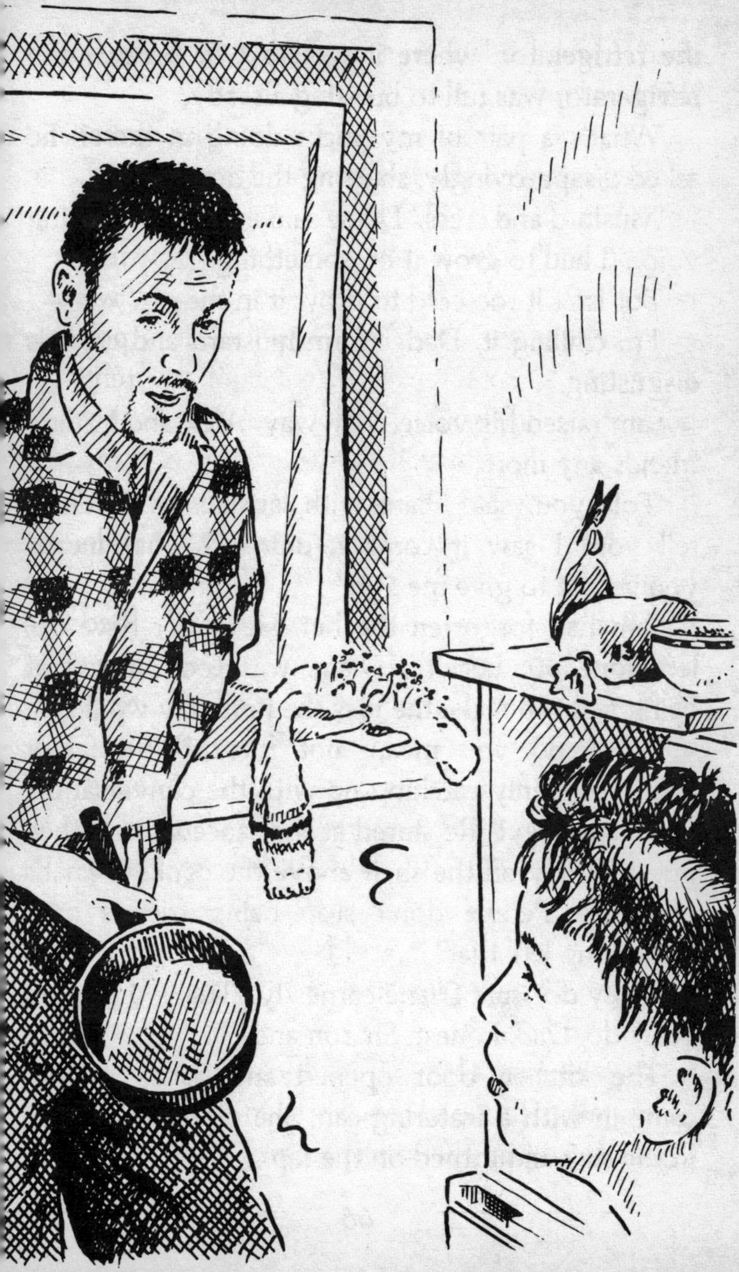

the refrigerator, where it wouldn't fit because the refrigerator was full to bursting already.

'What's a pair of my socks doing in there?' he asked disapprovingly, shutting the door again.

'Mustard and cress,' Diane said in a long-suffering voice. 'I had to grow it on something.'

'But isn't it too cold to grow it in the —'

'I'm chilling it, Dad. Warm mustard and cress is disgusting.'

Sam raised his voice. 'Anyway, Alex and I aren't friends any more.'

'Told you,' said Diane with satisfaction. 'Didn't I tell you? I saw it coming, didn't I? That means you've got to give me 50p.'

Sam had forgotten the bet. He didn't have 5p, let alone 50. Luckily, Diane was too pleased at being right to make the fuss she normally would.

'What do you mean, not friends?' his father asked, suddenly catching up with the conversation. 'You and Alex?' He stared at the saucepan and then put it briskly on the shelf above the cooker. 'That's nonsense. People don't stop being friends over something like that.'

'They do,' said Diane earnestly. 'That's the point. They do, Dad, honest. Sharon and I . . .'

The kitchen door opened and Sam's mother came in with a watering-can. She plonked it down in the sink and turned on the tap.

'I've done the back,' she announced. 'Your turn to do the front now. Do you know how many dandelions there are on the front lawn?'

'None?' Sam's father said hopefully.

She shook her head.

'One little tiny one, too small to notice?'

'Fifty-eight.'

Sam's mother handed over the dripping watering-can. Her husband departed looking stunned.

Sam could have followed him out to the garden to finish the story, but it was too much bother. He raised his voice above the clattering as Diane and his mother put away knives and forks, and began again.

'And Alex didn't speak to me after school,' he finished. 'I spoke to him. I said "Goodbye, Alex," but he didn't answer. He just went off with Pete without saying anything.' Sam looked very hard at a trickle of water on the draining-board. 'I expect he's best friends with Pete now,' he ended gruffly.

'Told you,' said Diane again. 'Told you best friends don't last for ever. Me and Clare . . .'

'Off you go,' her mother said in a definite voice. 'Clean your room, tidy your cupboard, do your homework, wash your hair, cut the grass. Go on, off you go!'

'All at once?' complained Diane. 'At this time of

night? My room *is* clean. I haven't got any homework.' She never had a chance to point out that she couldn't use the lawn-mower, there was no shampoo, and she couldn't open her cupboard to tidy it because the door was broken (all of which was perfectly true).

'Out!' her mother said again, in the kind of voice it isn't worthwhile to disobey.

Diane disappeared outside to lodge an official protest with her father. When she'd gone, Sam's mother sat down with him at the kitchen table.

'Maybe Alex didn't hear you say goodbye. Maybe he was in a hurry. You've been friends for a long time now. Don't stop being friends over nothing.'

There was a crumb on the edge of the table. Sam flicked it over the edge. '*I* haven't stopped being friends with *him*. *He's* stopped being friends with *me*. That's different.'

'Well . . .' Sam's mother thought for a while. 'I think you're wrong about you and Alex. But even if you were right, you have other friends, don't you? What about James?'

Sam rolled his eyes. 'James left two terms ago.'

'Or Sasha.'

'Sasha plays with Albert.'

His mother went on making suggestions. Sam went on shaking his head.

'Everyone's already got people to play with. Except me. I won't have anyone at all.'

'What about the new girl, the one you're looking after?' his mother said at last. 'She can't have made other friends already. Why not play with her while you get things straight with Alex?'

'Emma?' Sam stared. 'I don't want to play with her. She's a girl. She won't like the same things as me. I don't even know her.'

'Pretty silly to quarrel with Alex over her, wasn't it?' Sam's mother said, exasperated. 'And you shouldn't write her off as a friend just because she's a girl. Some girls are quite human.'

Sam shook his head. 'She can't talk properly. She keeps saying "yeth".'

'She's new. It's not easy being at a new school. You'd probably say yes to everything if it was your first day somewhere.'

'I wouldn't say "yeth", no matter how new I was.' Sam slid his chair back from the table. 'Or "thpathe monthterth". I want to look after Emma, but I'm not playing with her. It's out of the question.'

'Off you go,' his mother said rapidly. 'Tidy your room, have a shower, put your books away, feed your trainers, find your gerbil. Goodnight, Sam. Today has lasted long enough.'

'You said something rather silly then,' Sam pointed out after a mental check.

'That makes two of us, doesn't it?' she snapped back.

Sam gave her a dignified kiss to show he forgave her for being bad-tempered, and went upstairs.

Later on she came up to switch out his light.

As she bent over to give him a hug she said: 'Things will look better in the morning. They always do.'

'They don't, actually.' Diane stuck her head in through the door on her way to the bathroom. She had just finished helping her father recount the dandelions. The new total was seventy-one, which they both thought was probably a record. 'In the morning, things quite often look worse. I mean, take me and Amy —'

But before Diane had a chance to fill in the details, Sam's mother shut the door.

Seven

In Sam's case, Diane was right: in the morning things looked a whole lot worse.

For a start, the first thing Sam saw when he walked into school was Pete and Alex talking outside the dining-hall.

Diane shot off to look for Natasha, who'd been her best friend for a whole day. Sam's mother escorted Laura in the direction of the infants' cloakroom. Sam was left to hover on his own, wondering whether it would be a good idea to say hello to Alex. He had just decided that it would, when Pete said something to Alex, and Alex laughed.

Sam hadn't heard what Pete said. All the same, he thought it was probably something about him. So he walked straight past Alex without even a glance, and said hello to Albert instead.

Albert said hello back, but before Sam had thought of anything else to say, Albert spotted Sasha on the other side of the playground. Two seconds later, Sam was alone again.

When he turned round to see what Alex and Pete were doing, he saw Pete give Alex something. Sam was too far away to tell for certain, but it looked like a marble. Pete had a huge marble collection and he never gave any of it away to

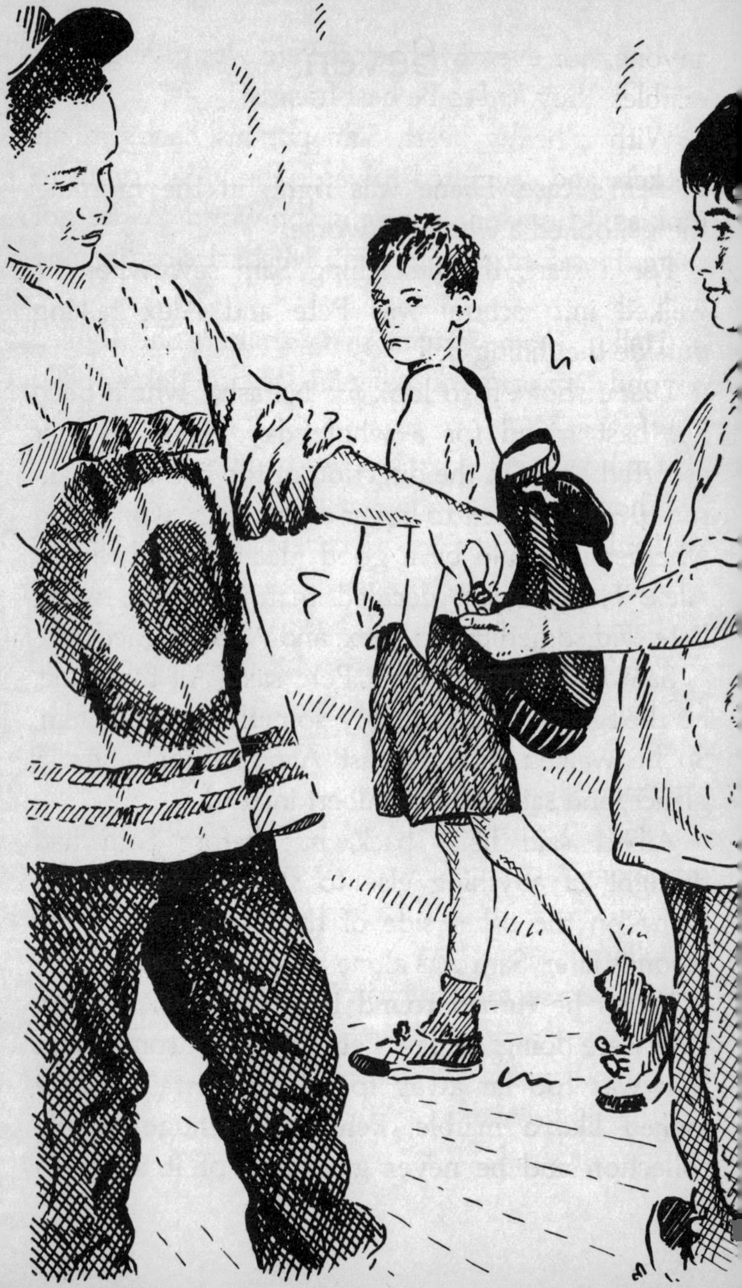

anyone, not even Michael. If Pete was giving Alex marbles, they *had* to be best friends.

With a heavy heart, Sam put his hands in his pockets and sauntered towards the gate, trying to look as if he hadn't a care in the world. As he got there, Emma turned up, with Michael close behind her.

'Hello, Tham,' Emma said, smiling. She looked beyond him and smiled again. 'Hello Alekth, hello Pete.'

'I'm here too, you know,' said Michael mildly.

'Thorry. I didn't thee you. Hello, Michael.'

'*I'm* looking after Emma today,' Sam said fiercely to Alex.

'I am too,' Alex snapped back.

Pete's head appeared over Alex's shoulder. 'And I'm helping Alex look after Emma!'

'If Pete's helping, I'm helping,' said Michael automatically.

Albert halted beside Michael. 'What's this? A game or something? I want to play too.'

'You can't. It's not a game,' cried Sam and Alex simultaneously.

Nobody seemed to hear.

'If Albert plays, I play,' Sasha stated, looming up on the other side of Michael. 'What are we playing, and bags I go first.'

'It's not a g—'

'Nobody goes f—'

They might as well have saved their breath.

Mary's head and shoulders popped up out of nowhere between Pete and Albert, swiftly followed by the rest of Mary. 'Bags you let us play too,' she announced.

'Who's "us"?' asked Sam, head spinning.

'Just me and Hannah. Oh, and Kate, of course.'

'And Amanda,' a small voice called from somewhere out of sight.

'And Amanda,' Mary finished. 'That's all, really.'

'All!' Alex cried. 'That's practically the whole class. It's practically the whole planet!'

'And I told you: we aren't playing a game anyway,' Sam said heatedly. 'We were only talking about who's going to look after Emma.'

'Emma?' Mary looked round. 'What's Emma got to do with anything? Emma isn't even here!'

'She is!' Sam looked wildly around. No Emma. 'She has to be. She was standing right there by Michael!'

Everyone looked at Michael.

'Why is everyone looking at me?' he asked. 'I don't know where she is. She went off hours ago.'

'Oh great!' Sam said bitterly. 'That's all I need. I've lost her!'

The bell rang.

Mary, Hannah, Kate and Amanda raced off to-

74

wards the classroom. Sasha and Albert strolled after them. Pete, Michael, Sam and Alex came last, arguing all the way.

'It's all your fault,' Sam told Alex fiercely. 'If you'd let me look after her the way I was supposed to, it would never have happened.'

'I'm supposed to look after her too!'

'So am I,' said Pete.

'No, you're not,' said Sam and Alex together.

Michael's face fell. 'If Pete's not looking after Emma, neither am I, then,' he said sadly.

'No one's asking you to look after Emma,' said Sam.

'You couldn't look after a wet paper bag,' said Alex.

'Neither could you, then,' said Pete coldly. He looked at Alex. 'And I want my marble back.'

Alex reached into his pocket and handed it over. They hung up their coats without speaking, but as they went into class Michael said: 'You should tie her up, that's what I think.'

'*What?*' said Sam.

'Or lock her in some place.'

'You're joking, aren't you?' said Alex.

'No. I mean, you could give her food and everything.' Michael's brow was furrowed with thought. 'You could even let her out once a day for exercise. With chains round her feet so she couldn't run away —' He broke off. 'What are you looking at me like that for? I'm only trying to help, aren't I?'

'Thanks,' Sam said wearily. 'I'd rather you didn't.'

Emma walked into class with Sally Platt, of all people.

'Over here, Emma,' Sam called, waving. 'I saved you a seat.'

'So did I!' called Alex.

'Thankth!' Emma sat down at their table. So did Sally.

'I didn't ask *her*,' Sam growled at Alex as Mr Dixon doled out maths worksheets.

'Some people!' Alex growled back.

'Are you two talking or working?' Mr Dixon enquired.

Sam did his best to help Emma with her maths, but he wasn't very good at it. Sally Platt, unfortunately, was *very* good indeed.

'Talk about showing off,' Sam muttered to Alex as Sally demonstrated how to take 19 from 51, and 37 from 93. 'Anyone can do *that*.'

'What's the answer, then?' asked Alex casually.

Five minutes and two sheets of scrap paper later, Sam said '32.'

Alex looked at him blankly. 'What?'

'The answer's 32,' Sam repeated.

'The answer to what?'

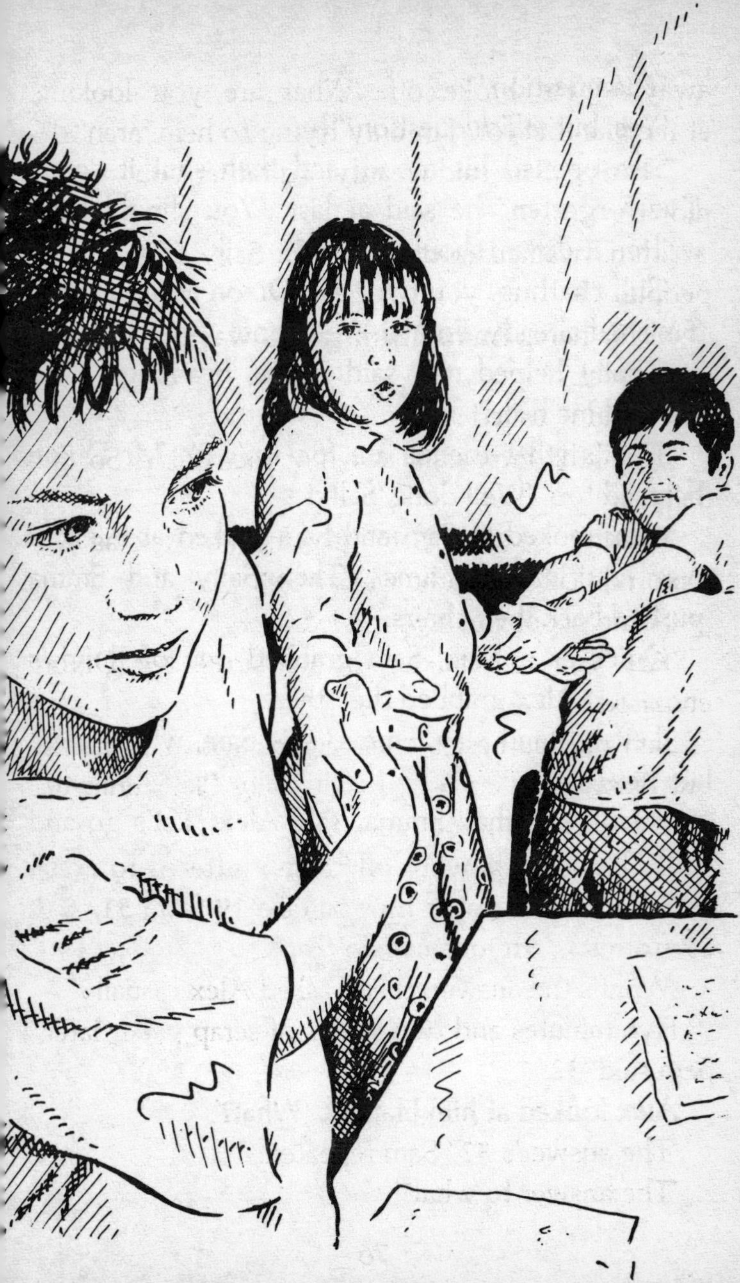

'The question.'

'Yes, but *which* question?'

Sam opened his mouth and then shut it again. 'I've forgotten,' he said at last. 'You should have written it down, shouldn't you?'

'Still chatting, you two?' Mr Dixon asked gently. 'Finished already, Emma? Well done!'

'Thally helped me,' said Emma, beaming. 'Thee thowed me how.'

'That's what friends are for, isn't it?' Mr Dixon beamed too. 'Well done, Sally!'

Alex looked at Sam and Sam looked at Alex. It was just like old times. Then Sally and Emma pushed back their chairs.

Quick as a flash, Sam grabbed one of Emma's arms and Alex grabbed the other.

'Let's go and play, Emma,' said Sam, with a glare at Alex.

'I tell you what, Emma,' said Alex. 'Let's go and play.'

Eight

Emma walked out into the sunshine between Sam and Alex. With Sam holding one arm and Alex the other, she didn't have much choice. They stopped in the middle of the playground.

Sam and Alex tried to figure out what to do next. Emma wriggled and said: 'Where'th Thally? can you thee Thally anywhere?'

Suddenly Sam had a brainwave. Skipping! That was the kind of thing girls liked. They were at it all over the playground sometimes. He and Alex often grumbled to each other about it. He and Alex . . .

Sam pulled himself up sharply. This was no moment to dwell in the past. Across the playground, he could see Diane skipping on her own. All he had to do was nip across and ask to borrow her skipping-rope. Surely she'd let him, just this once.

'Hold on to Emma,' he ordered Alex. 'I've got to get something. Wait here, Emma, and don't go getting lost again. I'll be back!'

A strange expression came over Emma's face. 'What do you mean, "Don't go getting lotht again"?' she asked crisply. 'I don't go getting lotht. I never have got lotht. What are you talking about, Tham?'

'I'll be back!' Sam shouted comfortingly as he tore off across the playground.

'What do you want?' Diane asked when he skidded to a halt in front of her. She wasn't so much skipping as swishing the rope this way and that.

'Nothing really.' Diane raised her eyebrows. 'Well, your skipping-rope, actually,' Sam said, coming clean. 'Since you're not using it, I mean. Can I borrow it to lend to Emma?'

There was a moody silence during which Sam held his breath. 'Why?' asked Diane eventually.

'Why? So she'll let me look after her, not Alex, of course.'

'Are you still not friends with each other, then?'

Sam shrugged to indicate that he didn't want to talk about it.

Diane nodded. 'You still like him, though, don't you?'

'Of course I do!'

Diane drew a circle on the playground with the toe of her well-scuffed shoe. 'Why don't you tell Alex that?' she said quite quietly.

Sam turned red with embarrassment. 'I couldn't do that,' he said in horror.

'Bet you could,' said Diane. She stopped staring at her shoe and looked him right in the eye. 'Bet you anything.'

'No, I couldn't,' Sam said again. 'And I bet you couldn't either. Now, please can I borrow the rope?'

'If you want.' To Sam's surprise she handed over the skipping-rope just like that.

'Thanks!'

'Bet you could, though,' she said again as he raced away.

Much to Sam's relief (because the whole thing had taken far longer than he had bargained on) Emma was still where he'd left her, firmly tethered to Alex. He took up his hold on her free arm.

'Would you like to use this skipping-rope, Emma?' he asked, confident of the answer.

Emma's arm wriggled. 'No thankth. I hate thkipping.'

'You what?' Sam was flabbergasted.

'I hate thkipping. I'm hopeleth at it. You go thkip if you want to.'

While Sam was trying to come to terms with the failure of his scheme, Alex had an inspiration. 'What about a game of hopscotch, then?'

Startled, Sam let go of Emma's arm. 'You can't play hopscotch!' he cried.

Alex turned red, but he said: 'I can!'

'He can't, Emma,' Sam shouted. 'Don't listen to him. He's never played hopscotch in his life.'

81

'I can learn, can't I?' Alex let go of Emma's other arm in order to argue properly. 'It's just kicking a stone and hopping. Come on, Emma. We'll play hopscotch.'

Alex reached for Emma's arm, and missed.

'I don't want to play hopthcotch,' Emma said, backing away. 'It'th thilly!'

Alex's jaw sagged.

'There!' Sam was relieved but cross.

'What do you mean "There"?'

'Emma doesn't want to play with you. I'm the one she wants to look after her.'

'Oh yes?' Alex's face was very fierce. 'When did she say so?'

'She doesn't need to say so. It's obvious!'

'Ask her then,' Alex said defiantly. He still felt the hopscotch idea had been a good one. 'See what she says!'

'Right,' Sam shouted. 'I will!'

'And I'll ask her too,' Alex shouted back. 'Emma . . . Emma? Where are you?'

Sam groaned. 'Oh no, not again!'

They searched the playground from end to end before Michael pointed Emma out. She was sitting on the grass at the edge of the football field, making a daisy chain.

Sam tied with Alex in the race to her side.

Michael came third, with Pete a step behind. After that came Sasha, Albert, Mary, Amanda, Julie, Kate, and just about everyone else in Sam's class.

'Who do you want to look after you, Emma — me or Alex?' Sam demanded, recovering his breath a split second sooner than Alex.

'It'th funny you thould athk that,' said Emma, inspecting a mangled daisy, 'becauth —'

'It has to be one of us or the other,' Alex interrupted. 'It can't be both.'

'And I've looked after you best,' Sam reminded her. 'I showed you round school yesterday, didn't I?'

'Yeth.' Emma dropped the mangled daisy on the grass.

'I helped you with your drawing though,' Alex said quickly. 'Remember that, Emma?'

'What? Oh, yeth.'

'I . . . I'll give you some of my crisps tomorrow if I'm looking after you,' Alex offered.

A murmur ran among the spectators. 'That's bribery,' said Pete with approval.

Sam turned pale. 'If I look after you, you can share my chocolate bar.'

'How big a share?' asked Julie.

Amanda nodded. 'Get it settled now,' she advised Emma, 'in front of witnesses.'

'She can share *all* my lunch,' Alex shouted.

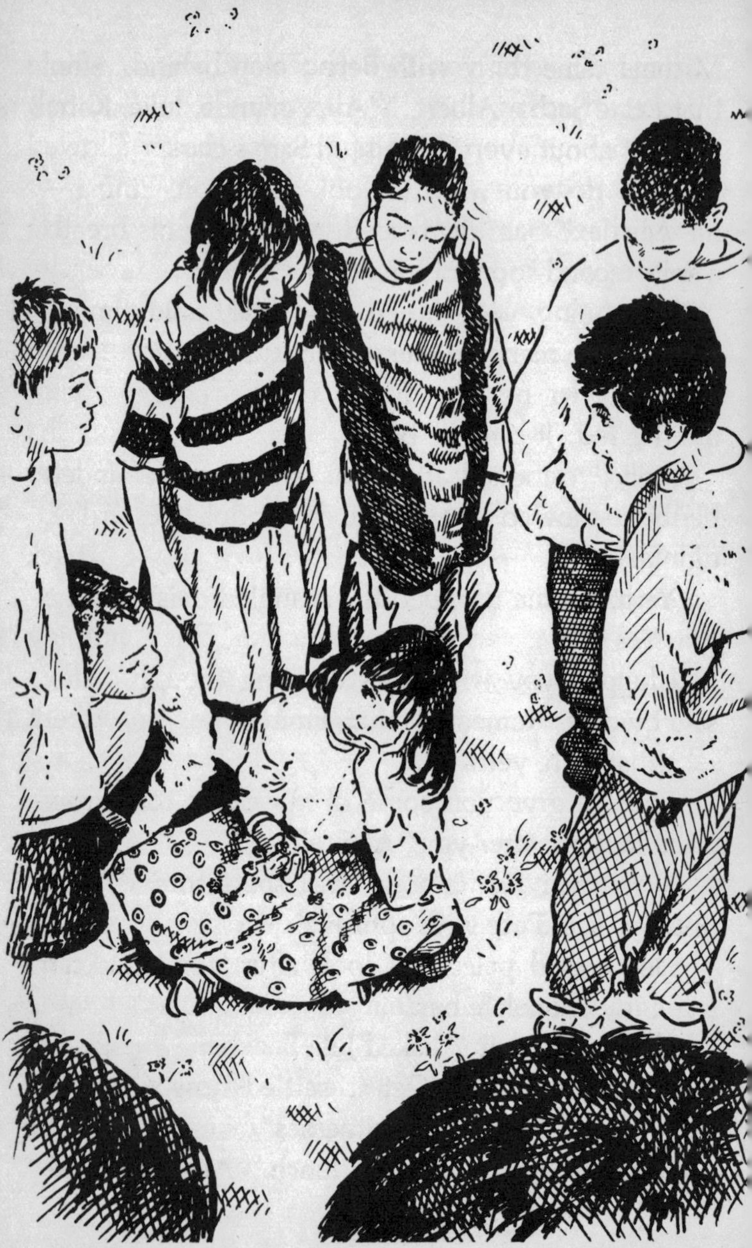

'Emma, I'll give you two chocolate bars, a whole packet of crisps, and...' Alex came to a dead halt as his imagination dried up. He was never allowed chocolate bars anyway.

Michael was the first to recover his voice. He stepped forward and tugged Alex's sleeve urgently. 'You can look after me, if you want to. My favourite crisps are cheese and onion. The chocolates I like are Mars bars and Twixes.'

'I'll take any sort of chocolate bar,' said Sasha rapidly. 'Make it three bars and you can look after Albert too. And my brother. And —'

'Get lost, Sasha!' Alex said. 'And you, Michael. I'm not giving any of you anything.'

'Yes, just go away!' Sam shouted. 'This is nothing to do with any of you!'

'I was only asking,' Sasha said. 'Come on, Albert. This is very boring.'

People began to drift off in different directions. Michael was the last to go.

'What's so great about looking after Emma anyway?' he asked plaintively over his shoulder as he left.

For the first time that day, Sam found himself really looking at Alex. They had been friends for so long that he suddenly felt he knew what Alex was thinking. And he was thinking the same himself:

What *was* so great about looking after Emma?

Was she worth it?

Was *anyone* worth it?

And all at once, Sam knew the answer.

'Just a minute —' said Sam.

'Emma, wait —' said Alex.

'Alex and I have to —'

'— talk to each other!' Alex finished.

'Go on, then,' Emma said, without looking up from her daisy chain. 'I'll thtay here. I'm waiting for thomeone.'

'Who's thumbwun . . .?' Sam began, but Alex's elbow prodded him gently in the ribs. 'Back in a minute!' he cried. 'Come on, Alex!'

As soon as they were round the corner of Mrs Parker's class, Sam stopped. 'I don't really mind if you look after Emma,' he told Alex. 'It's OK, honestly.'

'But I don't really mind if you look after her!' Alex said. 'I mean, Mr Dixon asked you first.'

'He asked you second.' Sam looked at his shoes. 'And I wish he'd never asked either of us. Then we'd still be friends, the way we used to be.'

'Aren't we friends?' Alex asked, surprised.

There was a pause. Then: 'I'm still friends with you,' Sam said in a small voice. 'I like you better than anyone. But I thought you and Pete were best friends now.'

'Pete?' said Alex. 'Pete's OK, but he's not my best friend. You're my best friend. You always have been.'

Sam stopped looking at his shoes and smiled a smile as big as Emma's. 'That's all right, then!' Suddenly, he had another brainwave. 'I tell you what: we'll share Emma. OK?'

'Done!'

They raced back together to the edge of the football field.

'Emma,' Sam began, panting from relief and running. 'You know we said you had to choose which of us was going to look after you?'

'Yeth?' Emma squinted up into the sunlight at them.

'Well, we've changed our minds. We're both going to look after you. You don't have to choose between us after all.'

Emma rose to her feet. She dusted grass and dead daisies off her skirt. She looked at Sam. She looked at Alex. She looked past them to someone else. Finally she spoke.

'Get lotht,' she said cheerfully. 'I can look after mythelf. I'm going to be betht friendth with Thally.'

Sam and Alex watched in silence as Emma and Sally walked away arm-in-arm.

'Well!' said Sam at last. 'After all we did for her!'

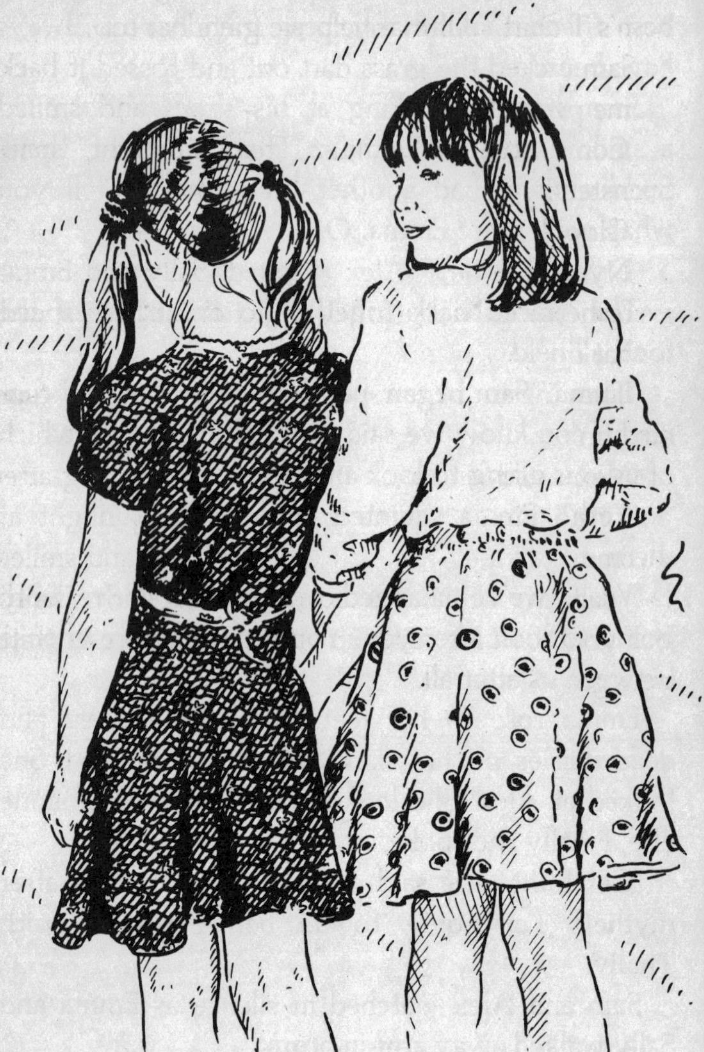

'It's unbelievable!' Alex aimed a grass dart at Sam's T-shirt. 'All that help we gave her too.'

Sam picked the grass dart out and tossed it back. 'Some people!'

'Come on, we've just got time for space monsters!'

'Gloop!'

'Nyugga – hey,' Alex stopped. Sally and Emma were heading back in their direction at high speed. 'What do they want?'

'They needn't think I'm changing my mind,' Sam said firmly.

Alex nodded. 'You won't catch me looking after anyone again.'

Emma skidded to a halt a metre away and smiled her dazzling smile. 'I'm betht friendth with Thally, but you can play with uth, all right? There'th thith new game I've invented. It goeth like thith . . .'

Nine

'That's *enough*, Sam,' said Mr Dixon. They were back in class. Playtime had ended early. 'Be quiet, Alex. How do you expect me to understand what you're saying when you all shout at once? No!' Mr Dixon clapped his hands to his ears. '*Don't* all try to tell me!'

When the noise had sunk to a few sobs and snuffles, Mr Dixon looked sadly round the classroom. 'I thought it was understood, absolutely understood by every single one of you, that there was to be *no more horrible hedgehog*.'

Everyone started to speak.

Mr Dixon held up one hand. 'All right, all right. If you weren't playing horrible hedgehog, what *were* you playing? And whose idea was it? Was it you again, Sally?'

Sally shook her head. 'No, Mr Dixon. It wasn't my fault, I promise.'

'Whose fault was it, then? Somebody must have started it. Sam, what do you know about this?'

Sam jumped and then looked hard at his shoes.

'Very well,' Mr Dixon said. 'What about you, Alex?'

Alex looked hard at the ceiling.

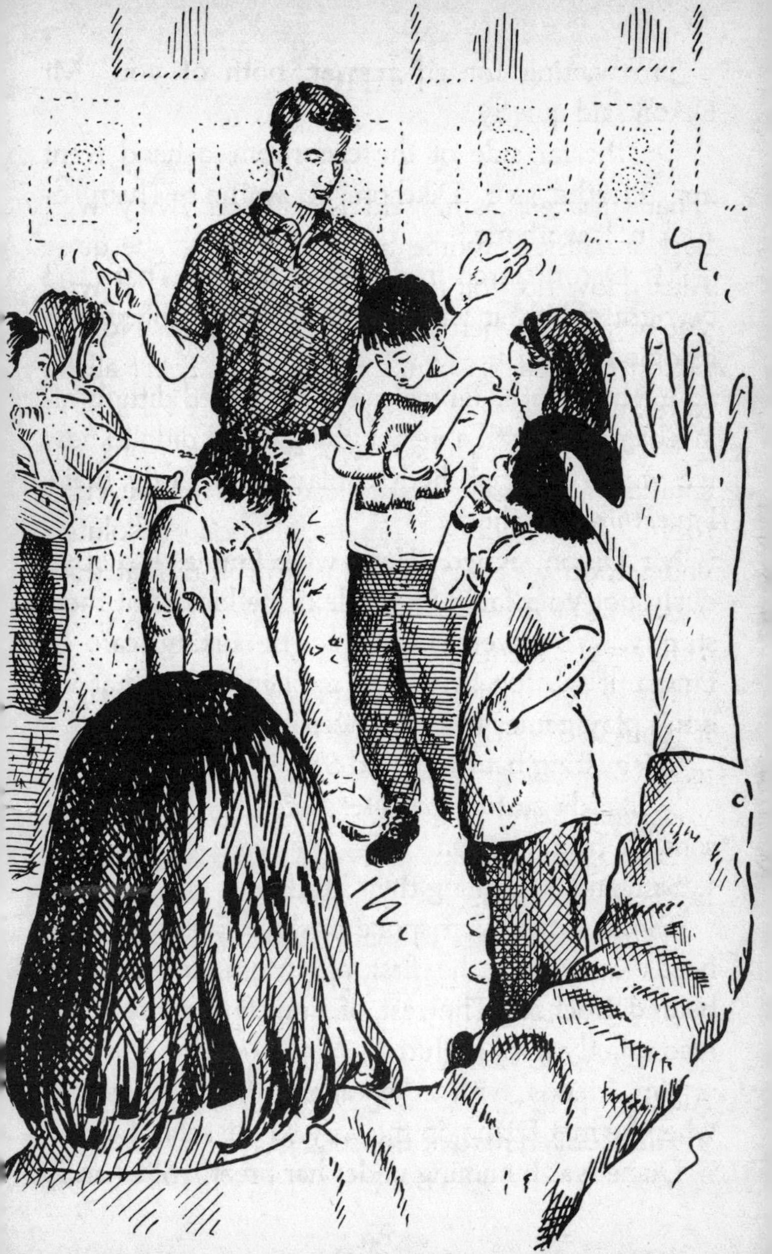

'I'm waiting for an answer, both of you,' Mr Dixon said quietly.

On the far side of the classroom, a hand went up. 'Pleathe, Mr Dikthon, it wathn't Tham or Alekth. It wath me.'

Mr Dixon stared in disbelief. 'Emma? That can't be right! Surely it wasn't you who thought up this terrible game?'

'Yeth, it wath,' Emma said. 'It'th called dithguthting hamthter. It'th a very nithe game. I didn't know we weren't thuppothed to play it. Nobody thaid. I'm *ekthtremely* thorry.'

Mr Dixon sighed. 'Very well, Emma. It's obviously not your fault. Sam! Alex!' He looked at them sternly. 'You were meant to be taking care of Emma. It was up to you to explain to her that we don't play games like whatever-it-was —'

'Disgusting hamster,' said Sam in a small voice.

'— like disgusting hamster here. Try to be more sensible from now on.'

Sam and Alex hung their heads.

'Right!' Mr Dixon spoke briskly. 'Everyone who needs to go to the first aid room, form a line behind Michael. The rest of you, find a book and read quietly until I return.'

'I'm friends with Alex again,' Sam announced when he met Diane on the way to the school gate.

Diane was humming under her breath. She hardly

looked down her nose at all as she said: 'Already? That won't last. You made up too quickly. You'll probably be quarrelling again tomorrow.'

'No, we won't — well,' Sam corrected himself, 'if we do, we'll still go on being friends. I mean, we quarrelled once, and now we're friends again. A quarrel isn't the end of everything.'

'That's true.' Diane sounded slightly surprised. 'Ruth and I have had millions of quarrels, but we're still best friends with each other. We always have been, really. I always liked her better than anyone else.'

'Told you so,' Sam said. It wasn't strictly true, but he knew when it was his turn to be right for a change.

On the way home, Laura gave a blow-by-blow account of her second day at school. Steven Maddox featured a fair bit in the story, but Malcolm-with-the-ears also had an unexpected role, as somebody Laura had been forced to hit over the head with her PE bag.

'Oh Laura!' her mother said sternly. 'I told you yesterday. No hitting!'

'But Malcolm asked me to,' Laura bellowed. 'He saw me hitting Steven and he said it wasn't fair, so I had to hit him with my bag as well. I explained all that to Mrs Hotchkiss *and* Mrs Parker *and* Mr Elliot *and* Mr Peabody.'

'You had to go to the Head?' Diane sounded impressed against her will.

'On your second day?' asked Sam. 'I suppose Mr Peabody gave you a biscuit too!'

'No,' Laura said crossly. 'Only a sweet.'

'Only?' Sam tried a bitter laugh, but it didn't come out properly, he was feeling too happy.

While his mother delivered her lecture on non-violence again for Laura's benefit, Diane said: 'You lost your bet, you know.' Seeing Sam look puzzled, she explained, 'You bet I couldn't tell someone I still liked them. And I did. And I bet you you *could*. So what happened? Did you tell Alex?'

'It wasn't really a *bet*,' said Sam hopefully. 'Was it?'

'Told you you could.' Diane grinned at him.

'Tell you what,' Sam said in a burst of confidence, 'I might be friends with Emma too. And Sally. She's not bad when you get to know her. While Mr Dixon took the others to first aid, we made up this game. It's called revolting rabbit. What you do is —'

Diane came down to earth. She was definitely not ready to let Sam get away with telling her something twice in five minutes.

'Having three friends never works,' she said grandly. 'I know what I'm talking about. You wait and see.'

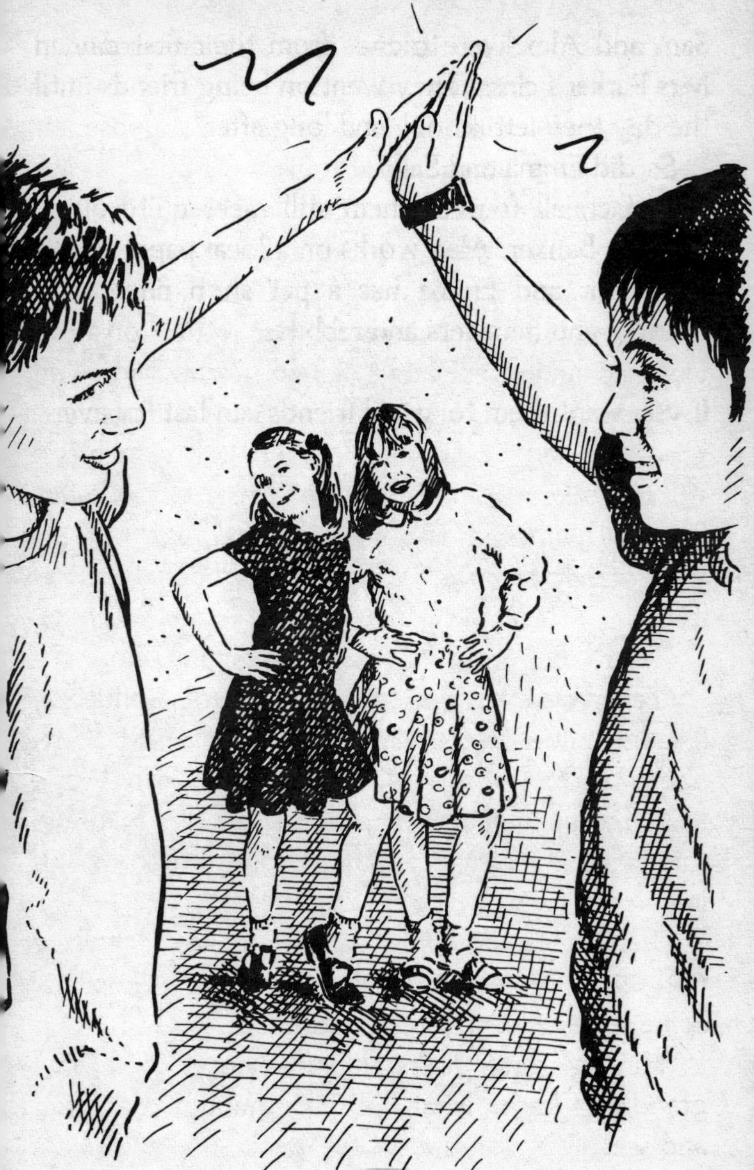

Sam and Alex were friends from their first day in Mrs Parker's class. They went on being friends until the day they left school, and long after.

So did Emma and Sally.

In fact, all four of them still meet quite often. Sally's a banker, Alex works on a local paper, Sam's a teacher, and Emma has a pet shop filled with children and hamsters and rabbits.

If you want them to, good friends can last for ever.